# relative strangers

GW00546746

Also by Gretta Curran Browne

**GHOSTS IN SUNLIGHT**

# relative
# strangers

## GRETTA CURRAN
# BROWNE

Payges Publishing Ltd
*PP*

RELATIVE STRANGERS
A novel by Gretta Curran Browne
Based on a screenplay by Eric Deacon
First published in Ireland by New Island Books

10 9 8 7 6 5 2

ISBN: 978 – 09558208-3-0

A CIP record for this title is available from the British Library.

Cover Design: Susana Liveras
Cover photo of Brenda Fricker by Dennis Mortell
Cover photo courtesy of Little Bird
Printed in England by CPI Cox & Wyman,
Reading, RG1 8EX

# ONE

The roar of the Aer Lingus jet as it descended towards the runway at Düsseldorf Express Airport was like an explosion of thunder in James Lessing's ears. A regular air traveller, he was not frightened, but he was hyped-up with anxiety because the flight had left Dublin an hour later than scheduled.

Now he too was running late. He would have to rush around like an athlete as soon as he landed and get his car out of the airport and onto the autobahn as quickly as possible.

Just the thought of it exhausted him. For too many years he had been rushing through life as if constantly ten minutes late for an appointment; terrified of missing out, terrified of being found out, always shadow-boxing with his shame while still delighting in the thrill of deceit.

Why had he done it?

Why had he even begun it?

Why had he not foreseen the complications and confusion it would cause? Why had he done this to himself?

He put a hand over the sudden pain in his chest — airline food always gave him indigestion. He lay back in his seat and closed his eyes. What was he to do? He was fifty years old and all he wanted now was to slow down, take stock, and possibly make some radical changes in his life. Perhaps even try and take his life back to how it had once been, sane and normal, without guilt, without so many callous lies.

The plane's wheels touched the ground and brought him back to earth. Back to Germany. Back to his home and family.

The azure sky above Rheindahlen looked down on scenes of pure tranquillity. A cricket match was in progress on one of the playing fields, while young children played their own games outside the boundary rope. A couple walking their dog stopped to chat to some of the watching players and their wives who were lounging on the grass. It all looked so English, so serene, it was hard to believe it was part of NATO headquarters.

Maureen Lessing worked in the Hospital of JHQ and she too was late for an appointment, hurrying anxiously down the busy corridor towards the conference room, still managing to smile and cheerfully acknowledge every person she passed on the way.

All the hospital staff, from senior doctors to junior porters, liked Maureen Lessing. A woman in her late forties, still very attractive, with blonde curly hair and beautiful eyes that were kind and honest and vividly blue. For five years she had been Major

2

Pinkerton's private secretary, and her warm personality and practical intelligence had inspired a great deal of affection and trust.

'Maureen …'

She turned and looked at an old prune-faced German gentleman who held out a red rose to her. It was Alfred, the man who ran the hospital's magazine and flower stall, a delighted grin on his face.

'Happy Birthday, Maureen,' he said. 'You see, romance is not dead.'

Maureen smiled ruefully. Until last night she had been forty-nine years old but feeling as young as a thirty-year-old, and now here was Alfred reminding her that today was her birthday, that another decade was behind her.

'So, how old today?' Alfred grinned. 'Twenty-one? Twenty-two?'

'Alfred,' she laughed, 'you are a real gentleman. Thank you.' She took the rose, kissed him and rushed on.

The meeting had already begun when she entered the conference room. She stared in dismay at the four officers already seated around the table, and smiled nervously.

'I'm sorry … I'm really sorry …' She quickly made her way round the table to sit next to her boss, wondering why her accent always sounded more Irish when she was flustered. She continued to apologise.

3

'Sorry, I just couldn't get —'

'Yes, well if we could all get on,' Brigadier Black cut her short. As the man who ran the hospital he was not very happy. He glanced down at the finance papers in his hand and continued from where he had left off.

'Empty theatres are not cost-efficient. It's a simple equation. If you can't justify them, you close them.'

'I'm sorry, sir, but I have to say this is absurd.' Major Pinkerton looked furious. He was the Director of Medical Services and had spent three frustrating years fighting the brigadier's cost-cutting programmes. But this latest one was ridiculous.

'We have a fully staffed hospital here, and yet you want to buy in outside services from the German hospitals in Düsseldorf ?'

'Yes I do, because it's cost-efficient and it makes sense. Now, this business of the Psychiatric Ward in future, all psychiatric care will be provided direct from Düsseldorf. It's unfortunate, but we really can't afford these services on Base any longer.'

Maureen couldn't restrain herself. 'But surely that will mean longer waiting times,' she blurted out. 'More travelling, a less sympathetic environment. I thought it was the job of the army to treat all job-related disorders as priority!'

The four officers stared at her — she was there primarily to assist, not to comment.

'I'm sorry,' she said more quietly, glancing at her

4

boss, 'but somebody's got to say something.' She glared at Brigadier Black. 'The patients here are not just service personnel, they're *people*. Sick people who urgently need help. And they shouldn't have to wait for that help to come from Düsseldorf .'

Fifteen minutes later, strolling together down the corridor, Major Pinkerton looked very pleased with his secretary.

'So, Maureen, what happened to discretion being the better part of valour?'

Maureen shrugged. 'Well, he thinks he can put a price tag on everything. Anyway, I'm a civilian, he can't court-martial me.'

'I think he would like to try.'

'I'm sure he would.'

Major Pinkerton sighed. 'Anyway, give me another couple of years and I'll be out of it.'

'You?' Maureen gave him a cynical smile. 'No way. They'd have to carry you out feet first. Besides, what would you do?'

'Oh, I don't know. Go back home … join a General Practice? Get a job in the NHS?'

'The NHS? God, talk about jumping out of the frying pan into the fire.'

'Like you, Maureen my love, I like a challenge.' Major Pinkerton stopped outside his office door. 'Right, we'd better get on.'

'Oh, listen — you know I'm going off early today?'

'Are you?' Pinkerton paused, bemused, his hand resting on the door handle.

'I *did* tell you, Major.'

'Did you?'

Maureen flushed, embarrassed. 'It's my birthday.'

'Is it?'

'Yes.'

'Ah, that explains it then.'

Major Pinkerton pushed open his office door and the room inside erupted with singing voices: '*Happy Birthday to you, Happy Birthday to you, Happy Birthday dear Maureen …*'

Major Pinkerton grinned at the stunned expression on Maureen's face. 'I knew there just *had* to be some reason for all these people congregating in my office.'

The room was packed with nurses, doctors and colleagues, German and English, all singing and clapping along.

Andrea, an attractive German nurse in her early forties, stepped forward and presented Maureen with a white iced cake. It read, *50 Today!*

Maureen was so touched she felt tears spurting to her eyes, but she fought them back with a laugh. 'Oh, look at that — *50* — isn't it just an awful number to put on any woman's birthday cake …'

James Lessing rushed through the airport car park towards his blue Audi. The sun reflecting on the sea of car roofs hurt his eyes. It was hot and he was sweating. The bag he was carrying was heavy. He stopped to take a deep breath, then rushed on.

When he reached the Audi he took off his jacket and tossed it onto the back seat. He put his bag in the trunk, but decided to keep his briefcase near him on the passenger seat. He checked his watch — *almost two hours late*. He took another deep breath, climbed into the car and phoned home on his mobile.

*Ring … Ring … Ring …* He counted twelve rings before clicking off. Nobody home. He then called the hospital.

'I'm sorry,' the telephonist told him, 'Mrs Lessing is not in her office.'

All a bloody waste of time. He slammed the car door and gunned the engine, winding down the window to suck in some air.

As he exited through the airport underpass he emerged into brilliant sunlight which again hurt his eyes, making his headache worse, and all exacerbated by the pain of indigestion in his chest from the airline food. Why did he always eat the plastic rubbish, the frozen and reheated sludge? Why did anyone eat it? To pass the time, that's why. To pass the bloody *time*. When people weren't wasting it, they were rushing to keep pace with it — bloody *time*.

He glanced again at his watch, and frowned … the face of the watch looked blurred, he couldn't see where the hands were pointing. The traffic on the autobahn was light, but the few cars he could see also looked blurred. James blinked ... confused .... What the hell was happening? Were his glasses steaming up in the heat?

He kept his right hand steady on the wheel and raised his left hand to quickly pull off his glasses and clean them against his shirt, surprised and even more confused when he put them back on and found his vision was still blurred.

He lifted his head to check his eyes in the rear-view mirror, and it was then the pain hit him like a train — his entire body arched in agony. His foot involuntarily slammed down on the accelerator pedal, shooting the car forwards in a scream of tyres that sent it slewing crazily from side to side, the needle on the speedometer moving higher and higher ...

The front bumper slammed violently against the bank of the motorway's hard shoulder and the Audi somersaulted in the air before landing on its crushed roof.

James Lessing's body was still strapped inside his safety belt, upside down. The contents of his briefcase had tumbled onto the dashboard and front window. Near to his unconscious face lay a flowery birthday card with red glossy words on the front, *To My Darling Wife*. The inside page was blank. He had not had time to sign it.

Bottles of champagne had been popped and glasses filled.

Maureen, her arms full of presents, accepted the toast from Major Pinkerton. She smiled at him fondly; he was a lovely man and a great boss.

She looked round the room at all her friends and colleagues and suddenly realised how lucky she was. Life had been very kind to her. She had a good husband and two smashing kids, a nice home, and some of the best friends and colleagues a woman could wish for.

She drank back her champagne and felt a red glow of happiness blush her cheeks. So what if she was now *fifty*? So bloody what! A half a century of living was something to celebrate, not lament.

She allowed Major Pinkerton to refill her glass with more champagne, her smile beaming as she turned to the gathering and raised her glass in salute.

'Thank you,' she said sincerely. 'I wasn't expecting any of this ...' Maureen gestured to the cake and the presents. 'So thank you all, thanks for wanting to celebrate today with me. And — ' she chuckled, 'thanks for making *me* want to celebrate it too!'

An Irish medic at the back of the room raised his glass and said cheerily, 'That's it, Maureen, you say it *loud, I'm fifty and I'm proud*!'

Everyone cheered, but Maureen could only laugh.

The Lessing's semi-detached, tastefully decorated home was in a pleasant suburban street in a good area of Monchengladbach, fronted by a neatly kept lawn.

Inside the house, the telephone was ringing again.

Maeve Lessing was oblivious to the sound, her fifteen-year-old face entranced as she stared at the television screen, her eyes riveted on the handsome young face of Ronan Keating as Boyzone pounded out their hit *Love Me For a Reason*.

A minute later, Maeve's nineteen-year-old brother Brian rushed into the room wearing a black T-shirt and boxer shorts, holding a pair of jeans in his hand. He grabbed the remote from his sister and switched the TV off, indicating to the ringing telephone.

'The phone. You want to pick up the bloody phone?'

Maeve snatched the remote back. 'You pick it up!' She turned the TV back on. 'It'll be for you anyway.'

'Says who?' Brian stared at her furiously. They were the typical teenage brother and sister. 'Look, I'm ironing my jeans, yeah?'

Maeve glanced up at him, pained. 'You don't iron jeans, Brian. Nobody irons jeans.'

Brian picked up the phone. 'Yeah … Oh hi, Mum. Listen, I promised I'd pick up Eva but I'm skint and low on petrol. Can you lend me some money to get some?'

Amidst the general hubbub in Major Pinkerton's office, Maureen waved goodbye to friends taking their leave as she spoke to Brian on the phone.

'Then go on the bus, Brian, like everybody else.'

'Do what?' Brian's voice was astonished. 'Oh, come on,' he said cajolingly. 'It's a celebration isn't it? And I mean, we *are* taking you out to dinner.'

'Your father is taking me. You're just coming along for the ride.'

Maeve's defiant voice blared down the line. 'Listen, Mum, I'm not wearing a dress, not even for your birthday, okay?'

'Heaven forbid.' Maureen's voice was wry. 'Okay, no dress, Maeve. But now listen, Brian …'

'Yeah?'

'There's a twenty mark note on the dressing table. I'll be home in half an hour. Andrea's giving me a lift. See you.'

Maureen put down the phone and turned smiling to Andrea. 'Kids! I thought it was supposed to get easier.'

Inside the car on the drive home, Andrea glanced at Maureen with a dubious expression on her face. 'You wouldn't catch me going out for a celebration with my kids.'

'Oh, I don't know …' Maureen murmured. 'I like it.'

'But it's your birthday. What about romance, girl? Holding hands across the table. Champagne. Candle light.'

'We're probably going to a pizzeria,' Maureen cut in dryly. 'James isn't very big on eating out.'

Her stomach tightened at the thought of the dinner later that evening. It may have been her birthday, but would James even order wine? Over the past year or so he had become desperately mean, always trying to find ways to save money, dispensing with the first course in restaurants and ordering nothing better than the house wine.

If he was short of money, she could understand his new habit of penny-pinching, but according to Hans Reiner, James's accountant, the business was doing very well.

'What's that?' Andrea's eyes were fixed on the road, frowning at the flashing lights of police cars and an ambulance further ahead on the autobahn. 'Looks like an accident.'

Andrea slowed as they approached the police cars and the upturned wreckage of the blue Audi with its crushed roof and shattered windscreen. '*Scheisse*,' she muttered. 'That looks bad.'

Maureen's face blanched as she stared at the Audi. 'Stop the car.'

'What ?'

'*Stop it!*' Maureen shouted.

The police and medics had managed to get the driver's body out of the wreckage and lay it on a stretcher. One of the medics glanced up at a policeman.

'Identification? Anyone know his name?'

'James Lessing …' Maureen said.

The policemen and medics stopped and turned to her. Maureen stood ashen, her blue eyes wide with disbelief as she stared at the blood-stained man lying on the stretcher.

'You know him?' a medic asked her.

'He's my husband …'

A moment later Maureen felt the comfort of Andrea's arms around her.

# TWO

The house was deathly silent. It was the darkest and loneliest time of the night.

Maureen sat at the kitchen table in her dressing gown, staring at a plastic bag containing all of James's personal affects. He had still been alive when they reached the hospital, but all efforts to save him had failed.

James … she couldn't really believe that he was dead. It was like a bad dream. Twenty-two years they had been married, but it seemed as if she had known him all her life. So how could he be dead?

Tears gushed into her eyes at the pain of his loss. He hadn't phoned her from Holland and she hadn't tried to contact him. They had made the old, marital mistake of taking each other for granted, thinking they had years ahead together, always thinking there would be plenty of time to chat and catch up with each other's news when he got back.

All those damned business trips!

The tears rolled over her lids and spilled down her face. Why had he insisted on making those trips away so often? All for money? Wasting so much of the time they should have been spending together.

'It's my work,' he had kept saying. 'It's my work. It's what keeps the roof over our heads.'

Sometimes he had gotten very angry about it, his voice rising to a belligerent shout. 'Maureen, it's the 1990s and everyone *has* to work hard to survive! To keep in the race. What the hell do you expect me to do — sit back and retire? With two kids to provide for?'

In the end she had stopped arguing with him and accepted the necessity of his business trips. Now she wished she hadn't. Now she wished she had tried harder to make him spend more time at home with her. Because now he was dead and there was no more time left.

She wiped a hand over her wet face and, despite the heat of the kitchen, she shivered.

Finally, reluctantly, she lifted the plastic bag and emptied the contents onto the table ... James's handkerchief, neatly folded as usual. His glasses — one lens badly cracked ... House keys. Mobile phone. Cigarettes. Some loose change. His wallet ... an Aer Lingus ticket to Dublin ...?

Maureen paused, confused. Dublin? She was sure he had been in Holland. Didn't he say he was going to Holland? Slowly she shook her head and put a hand to her forehead, unable to think. Nothing seemed to make sense anymore.

Again she shivered, and closed her stinging eyes, wishing she could pray. But it was too late for praying, too damn late.

Major Pinkerton entered his office on the dot of 8.30 a.m., as always. He dropped down his briefcase and stood for a moment staring at the wall behind his desk covered in a montage of "Thank You" cards and messages from grateful patients.

'Maureen's Wall' he secretly called it, because she had been the one who had come up with the idea, indeed had insisted, a year earlier, that every card or note be pasted on his wall.

'To remind you,' she had asserted, 'that despite all the other problems connected to this hospital, it's *the patients* who count, and *the patients* who really *do* appreciate all the work you do on their behalf. So buck up and to blazes with Brigadier Black!'

Dear, dear Maureen. He wondered how she was coping?

He exhaled heavily and stood staring at her colourful wall. And what's more, he wondered, how on earth was *he* going to cope while she was away?

A sound from the connecting office made him turn his head, startled.

He walked over to the dividing door and opened it … the floor was covered with dozens of files. Maureen was on her knees, arranging and weeding out papers prior to putting the files back inside the various open filing cabinets.

'Maureen! For God's sake. What are you doing? You shouldn't be here.'

Maureen didn't even look at him, her voice flat. 'I'm fine, honestly.'

'No, you're not.'

Maureen ignored him and carried on her work with the files. 'Besides,' she said quietly, 'this filing system is in a real mess.'

'Bugger the filing system!' The major blocked her protest. 'No! I'm serious, Maureen. The bloody files can wait. I don't want you here. Not for at least a week. Not until after the funeral. Do you hear me?'

After an awkward moment of silence, Maureen finally rose to her feet. She gazed at him with such a white, ravaged face, lined with tiredness and grief, he had to look away from her.

He turned and lifted her coat from a hook behind the door and handed it to her. She stared back at him as if he was taking away her last chance of maintaining some kind of saneness in her life.

'Go home, Maureen,' he said gently. 'Get drunk. Cry yourself to sleep. Anything — but go home. Okay?'

Maureen left the hospital and went straight to the funeral director's. The visit was a painful one. She could barely speak as she selected James's coffin, but she ordered the best, nothing but the best. The cost was enormous. How better it would be if all this money was being spent on a nice holiday for her and James instead.

But no, he had never had the *time* to take a holiday. Together. Not for years. Now it was too late.

Maureen came out of the front door of the funeral director's and rushed across the road — just seconds too late to catch the departing bus. She stared after it in dismay, a sudden feeling of exhaustion drooping her shoulders.

Damn it! Now there would be a wait of at least twenty minutes before another bus came along.

She stood on the pavement gazing idly about her. A sign above a shop window suddenly caught her eye, a sign she must have seen a thousand times before and never noticed — DRIVING SCHOOL. Oh now, she thought, wasn't that clever … establishing the office of a Driving School right behind a bus top.

She took a few steps forward and stood staring into the dark window, seeing nothing but her own reflection staring back at her. She spent some time critically examining her reflection, hating every middle-aged aspect of it, and thinking it ironic and cowardly that she had allowed herself to reach the age of fifty without learning how to drive a car.

In a spurt of rage at herself she walked up to the driving school door and pushed it open. A young man sat behind a desk, an instant smile snapping onto his face as she walked inside.

'Can I help you?' he asked her.

'I want to learn how to drive,' she said angrily. 'And I want to learn fast.'

When Andrea called later that afternoon, she found Maureen upstairs in the bedroom laying out all of James's clothes and packing them neatly into black plastic bags.

Andrea was surprised and concerned. 'Are you sure you should be doing this?' she asked.

Maureen shrugged. 'They're just clothes, Andrea. But they're good clothes, too good to waste. I may as well let someone else have the benefit of them.'

'I'll help you,' Andrea said, lifting a jacket from the bed and folding it. 'How are the kids taking it?

'Oh, very quiet,' Maureen replied. 'Maeve looks lost, but it's hard to know what Brian is thinking or feeling. He takes after his father.'

'Not like Maeve.'

'God, no.'

'Maeve is a clone of you,' Andrea said. 'Still got the "Irish" in her.'

'Yeah,' Maureen smiled wryly. 'Worse luck. Last week she called her headmaster a middle-class misogynist — to his face!'

Andrea mused teasingly. 'I wonder where she gets it from?'

Maureen had turned back to the wardrobe. 'I never knew James had so many clothes.' She paused. 'But then ... these past few years, I didn't really know that much about him, did I?'

19

Andrea was so surprised she stopped folding and stared. 'Excuse me?'

Maureen turned and saw the expression on Andrea's face. 'Don't be shocked. James had his work, I found mine.'

She laid more clothes on the bed. 'Don't get me wrong, I enjoyed going out to work, and it was something to occupy me when he was away. But the truth is, the computer business was really James's life. And these past six or seven years, well … to be honest, James had little time to spare for me.'

Although Andrea was familiar with the Irish and their candour, so similar to Americans, she was nevertheless shocked by this sudden frankness from Maureen about her husband.

Andrea tried to think of something comforting to say. 'Well, you know, I suppose it was a big step when he left Ericsson's and went into business on his own.'

'It was, yes, a very big step,' Maureen agreed, feeling a sudden stab of guilt at her own selfish thoughts. 'And James was so desperate to succeed. To prove himself. The long hours he put in. He was always either locked off in his study or away somewhere drumming up business. I suppose we just grew apart … Yes, I suppose we did.'

Andrea didn't know what to say.

'He forgot our last two wedding anniversaries,' Maureen said. 'And as for my birthday, well, I searched through all the things in his travel-bag, and he *had* bought me a card, but he obviously hadn't found the time to buy me a birthday present … And yet, you know, there was a time, up until a few years ago, when the last thing James would have forgotten was our wedding anniversary or my birthday.' Maureen sighed bitterly. 'And all because of that damned business of his.'

Andrea was even more surprised by this disclosure. But, strangely, the realisation that Maureen's marriage had not been as perfect as Andrea had always thought it was comforted her.

Twice married, with two acrimonious divorces behind her, Andrea had always envied Maureen and her stable long marriage. But now she realised that all through the five years they had been friends and colleagues, Maureen had probably been even lonelier than herself.

Maureen suddenly looked at Andrea with puzzlement. 'Do you know, I didn't even know James was in Ireland. I thought he was in Holland somewhere. I'm sure that's what he told me.'

'What's going on?' Brian stood in the doorway watching his mother, a bewildered expression on his face. 'Mum, what are you doing?'

'Oh …' Maureen gestured vaguely with her hand. 'I wasn't sure what else to do with all your father's clothes. So I was just packing some of the best stuff to give to Oxfam.'

'*Oxfam!*' Brian stared at her as if she had gone mad. 'Dad isn't even buried yet! For Christ's sake,

Mum show him some respect!' Brian wheeled around and stormed off.

Andrea stared after him, while Maureen stood gazing down at the clothes lying on the bed for a long moment.

'He's right,' she said quietly. 'I should have waited. But I just wanted something active and positive to *do*, something that would take the edge off the awful reality of it all. Something that would stop me thinking ... and feeling.'

Andrea nodded, she understood, but she was also annoyed. Couldn't Brian *see* how upset his mother was? How devastated? Or was Brian like most men that Andrea had met, too engrossed in his own grief and self-pity that he couldn't see anything beyond his own thoughts.

Maureen looked confused, as if not knowing whether to stop packing or carry on. She stared at the clothes on the bed, then at the wardrobe, then all around the room ... Then she said something completely unexpected.

'Do you know, Andrea, someone in the hospital corridor today gave me their condolences, then tried to cheer me up by telling me I would probably be married again before long. Can you believe that?'

Andrea tutted with disgust. 'Some people are so tactless.'

Only now was Maureen feeling the anger of it. 'I mean what a thing to say! And Brian is right — James isn't even buried yet.' She grabbed up the black plastic bag full of clothes and pushed it back inside the wardrobe.

'People used to say that kind of thing to me,' Andrea said. 'But in my case it was different, I wasn't widowed, just divorced.'

'Would *you* ever get married again?' Maureen asked her seriously.

Andrea shook her head very definitely. 'No way. Never again. I don't need a man to clean up after. I've done all that, thank you very much. Besides, how do you say, "twice bitten, twice shy"? No, I've got my daughter; she's all I need. My daughter and my friends.'

Andrea looked at Maureen with true sadness in her eyes. 'And you are my best friend, Maureen, the one I like the most. And right now I want to cry because I feel so sorry for you.'

Maureen nodded, as if understanding, but her eyes were moving around the room again. 'All this …' she murmured, 'packing away James's clothes … none of it seems real, does it? Just a bad dream.'

The awful reality of James's death flared up again with relentless pain at the funeral mass.

Outside, the orange orb of the sun was rising high above the trees, but inside St Peter's Catholic Church the atmosphere was dark and quietly respectful.

Major Pinkerton and most of Maureen's colleagues from the hospital were present.

Maureen's sad eyes were on her children, especially Maeve who was crying silently and relentlessly. Dressed in black, her long brown hair tied back, Maeve looked older than her fifteen years. In height and physical development she could pass for sixteen or even seventeen, but inside she was still just a young girl of fifteen, frightened and bewildered and crying pitifully at the loss of her daddy.

Maureen longed to reach out and hug Maeve in motherly love, but decorum dictated that she remain in her seat, controlled and dignified, at least until the funeral was over.

Sitting beside his mother, Brian Lessing wore a black suit and a black tie, and although his heart was breaking, he was determined not to be pessimistic or mournful. He was determined to be as strong as his father had always been, and show this congregation that he could take the blow of his father's death and still stand like a man.

The priest finished the opening prayers and looked over at Brian.

Brian stood and walked up to the lectern, hunching rather self-consciously over a microphone that had been set too short for him.

'Someone sent us a letter … about Dad …'

Maureen sat, her face full of compassion, watching her nineteen-year-old son. Brian had idolised his father. And the two of them had always been so similar, the same dark-red chestnut hair, the same beautifully modulated voice, clear and deep.

'The letter said we should think about dying like the sun disappearing over the horizon,' Brian continued. 'It's sad when it's gone, but you know at that very moment it's appearing somewhere else … I'd like to think of my Dad like that … he's somewhere else now.'

Brian's resolve broke down at that point. He stood fiddling with the microphone; then suddenly moved away from the lectern and returned to sit beside his sister Maeve and his girlfriend Eva.

His mother sat on the other side of him. Her hand reached out and clasped his. 'Your father would have been so proud of you today,' she whispered.

Brian was not so sure about that, because a swamp of childish tears was gushing down his face.

The house in Monchengladbach was packed with people, noisy with the sounds of Irish, English and German accents. The atmosphere was more like a party than a funeral. The worst part was over. All anyone could do now was relax and try to cheer each other.

Brian moved through the gathering pouring little tots of whiskey into the women's tea cups. He smiled at an elderly German lady. 'We have schnapps if you prefer?'

'No. No,' she replied. 'Whiskey is good. Thank you …' she held up her tea cup for more.

An Irishman approached Brian from behind. 'Listen, son, you don't have any "Irish" there, do you?'

'No, it's Scotch,' Brian said politely. 'But I can get you some Irish from the kitchen. We have Jamesons.'

'Ah, good lad. But sure the Scotch'll do grand while I'm waiting — pour some in there.' He held out his glass and Brian began to fill it.

'Whoa! — not that much. I'm a cab driver so I drink only on my days off, and not too much of it either. But when I *do* have a drop, I like the best. Cheers!'

Brian smiled at the man, wondering who he was? He looked to be in his mid-forties, with curly dark hair turning grey, and smiling blue eyes.

Brian instantly divined that he was a man with a natural and good sense of humour, but other than that … Of course, being Irish, the man had to be a friend from his mother's side.

'You did well in the church today, Brian,' he said. 'I couldn't get over how tall you've grown. And she's looking well herself, considering …' They both glanced over at Maureen, locked in conversation with Major Pinkerton.

On the other side of the room, Maeve Lessing

was nervously watching her brother. Andrea stood beside Maeve holding a tray of sandwiches. 'He did all right, didn't he?' Maeve said, nodding towards Brian.

Andrea smiled fondly at the teenage girl, just a year older than her own daughter. 'Yes, he did. And so did you, Maeve. You both did very well.'

'Yeah. Well … Yeah.' Tears suddenly sprang into Maeve's eyes. 'We'll be all right, you know. Even though Dad's gone … we'll be all right.'

She said it more like an uncertain question than a definite statement.

'Hey, of course you will,' Andrea said reassuringly, putting an arm around Maeve's shoulder and giving her a small squeeze of comfort.

Maeve glanced over at her brother again and suddenly grinned. 'Look at Brian, look at his face! He's pretending not to be, but he's all confused. I don't think he has a clue who Sean is.'

Sean Mullen had also finally realised this fact. He stood looking at him with a shrewd expression on his face. 'You don't remember me, do you?'

Brian confessed, 'No, I don't.'

'That's because you haven't seen us since you were ten or eleven. But your sister Maeve — she comes over regularly in summer and stays with us in Dublin, doesn't she?'

'Ah, yes …' Brian nodded, recognition of the man's identity finally dawning.

Sean Mullen held out his hand. 'So, Brian, say

hello to your Uncle Sean. Well, really I'm a cousin, but anyway, who cares ...' He pointed towards a grey-haired woman in her seventies coming towards them. 'And that there is your Auntie Bridget.'

'Your wife,' Brian concluded.

'Wife! Are you blind or joking or what? Do I look that old? She's seventy-three and looks every day of it. She's me *mother*.'

Bridget Mullen had reached them. She quickly kissed Brian's cheek and then swopped her empty glass for the full glass in Sean's hand. 'Hello, Brian, how are you?'

'Oh, fine ... Auntie Bridget,' Brian answered with a swallow.

'I'm your *Great Auntie*. And you should come over to Dublin yourself and see us sometime, Brian. And bring that mother of yours. We haven't seen either of you in an age.'

'Oh, right ... I will.'

'It was a lovely funeral, so it was, and you have a grand turnout for such a sad occasion. But then it takes a tragedy to bring out the best in people I always say ... And haven't you got a lot of Japanese here in Germany?'

'Well please God your father is in a better place now,' Sean Mullen quickly interjected before his mother said too much. 'Nora. Nora, come here ...'

Nora Mullen was in conversation with another guest, but that didn't stop Sean grabbing her arm and pulling her towards Brian.

'Now *this* is my wife,' Sean said. 'This is Nora. She and your mother grew up together in Dublin. Best friends they were. Inseparable. Like sisters. Weren't you, Nora?'

Nora Mullen was a homely looking woman in her late forties. She had a soothingly soft voice when she spoke to Brian. 'Your father would have been very proud of the words you said about him.'

Brian smiled awkwardly. 'Thank you … Did you know my father?'

'We met him only the once. When he got married to Maureen.'

'Sandwiches anyone?' Andrea interrupted, holding out her tray.

'Oh God yes, I'll have one of those, I'm famished.' Auntie Bridget lifted a sandwich and examined it dubiously. 'Is that ham?'

'Ham, yes.'

'Are you sure?' Bridget adjusted her glasses and looked closely at the sandwich in her hand, inspecting it like a detective. 'It looks very red.'

'It's *German* ham, smoked,' Andrea replied. 'Try it — it's delicious.'

Nora Mullen cut in. 'Andrea, do you know where Maureen is?'

Andrea looked around her, unsure. 'In the kitchen, I think.'

Nora broke away towards the kitchen only to be intercepted by Maeve who grabbed her and hugged her. 'Thanks for coming, Nora.'

'Ah, darling …' Nora hugged the girl fondly. 'Nothing would have kept me away … not at a time like this.'

In the kitchen, Maureen was making more pots of tea and coffee when Hans Reiner entered, closing the door on the din from the lounge. Hans was a large man in his fifties who was prone to be somewhat reserved and ill-at-ease in a crowd.

He rushed to Maureen's aid. 'Let me do that.'

'No, thanks, Hans, I prefer to keep busy. It's therapeutic.'

'It's getting quite lively out there.'

Maureen smiled. 'That's the Irish contingent. My cousins.'

'It's good to have friends from home,' Hans said softly. 'After so many years away, do you still think of it as home? Ireland?'

'I don't know. I left there a long time ago …'

Maureen thought back to her early years in Dublin. She had left when she was twenty-one years old to work as a medical secretary in a London hospital, meeting James a year later. An Englishman who had romanced her off her feet. She had adored them both, James and London, and would have been happy to live in England for the rest of her life. But, of course, like most Irish people, she had always enjoyed those brief little holidays back in Ireland. Quick trips that had stopped once they had moved to Germany with James's new job at Ericssons.

Maureen looked up at Hans. 'Is Ireland still my home?' She smiled. 'It's always in the blood I suppose. Like being German.'

Hans said quietly. 'I should miss you, Maureen, if you left Germany now.'

She was surprised by this small intimacy, coming from a man like Hans.

Nora Mullen popped her head round the door. Maureen immediately smiled in true delight. 'Ahhh, speak of the Irish. Hans — this is Nora, my oldest friend. Nora, this is Hans Reiner. He was James's accountant.'

Both greeted each other and a second later Maureen was hugging Nora tightly, the two women almost sobbing with emotion.

'It's been so long,' Maureen said. 'Oh Nora, I'm *so* glad to see you.'

Hans stood ill-at-ease. 'Well, I'm due back at the office …' He quietly left the kitchen.

Nora eased back, wiping a tear from her eye. Maureen did the same and tried to laugh. 'Oh God, Nora, don't you start crying too.'

'Sorry,' Nora smiled. 'All that whiskey on an empty stomach.'

'Dutch courage, eh?'

'Well, you know, with rushing from the airport to the church. And then the sadness of the service and everything. I tell you, I needed something. I really don't know how you got through it, Maureen.'

'Valium. But don't tell the priest. He thinks it was his pep talk.'

Maureen gazed at Nora with a tearful haze of genuine appreciation in her blue eyes. 'I'm so glad you came, Nora. I know I'm not great at keeping in touch, but you know that you're the nearest thing to a family I've got left.'

Sean's voice broke in on them. 'God help you, Maureen. If we're the best you can do for a family.'

Sean Mullen stood smiling in the doorway. Maureen was already laughing as she turned to him. 'And who says I was including you, Sean Mullen?'

Long after midnight that night the house was in darkness save for a single light that shone from the lounge window, where Maureen was doggedly hoovering the carpet, oblivious to the noise she was making.

At 6.20 a.m., she wiped the last of the work surfaces clean and turned to survey her spotless kitchen. This compulsion to work non-stop and keep herself busy was not only irrational, it was exhausting her.

But something in the dark recesses of her mind was trying to push through to the surface, and she didn't want to hear it. She was afraid of something, but what was it? Keeping active was the only remedy for her troubled mind.

And yet … when she walked down the hall and reached James's study she could not resist stopping to stare at the closed door. There was a sign on it: *No entry. Man at work.*

She hadn't been inside that study for years. Entry was something James resented. His study was his private sanctuary, his own haven of peace away from the noise and interruption of the children.

But now all those rules were gone, the sign unnecessary, the study empty.

Maureen pushed the door open and walked inside.

Immediately she felt uncomfortable in this room that had never been a part of her domain — a working office, still in a state of organised chaos. Computer software journals and magazines were stacked on shelves, invoices and schedules pinned onto corked walls. Documents and letters still littered the desk around the computer.

Maureen turned and left the study, returning moments later with the hoover.

No, first she would make a start on the desk. She began picking up and neatly stacking the documents and letters into separate files. She inserted the documents in the top drawer for safe-keeping. But when she tried to open a second drawer for the letters — it was locked.

For a moment she stood puzzled; then had an idea. She took the key from the first drawer and tried it in the lock of the second — it worked.

Opening the drawer she saw it was full of bills … dozens of them. She pulled the piles out and began to sift through them — many of the bills had been left unopened. But those that had been opened … She stared at each one in disbelief, still unable to take it all in …

Two hours later she was still in the study, kneeling on the floor, the entire carpet strewn with letters and bills … James's software company owed money to absolutely everyone. The bank, suppliers, customers. The bills and threatening letters stretched back months.

'Mum,' Maeve called. 'Mum!'

Maureen could hear nothing but her own thoughts. How could this have happened? How could she have not known? Why had he not told her?

She went through the accounts book and searched again for some kind of answer. The company had made money over the years — lots of money — so where had it all gone?

'Oh, you're here,' Maeve said.

Maureen quickly turned away, gathering up the bills to hide them. 'Yes, I was just clearing up.' She gave a small laugh. 'The rubbish he collected.'

'Yeah.' Maeve looked quizzical. 'Mum, there's some guy at the door. He says he's come to give you driving lessons.'

# THREE

'The mirror. Check the mirror, Mrs Lessing …
Relax, you are very tense ….'

The driving instructor's voice sounded miles
away, somewhere along the edge of that reality she
was trying to block off … If the business was in so
much debt, with so many outstanding bills, then it
could only mean one thing — creditors, queuing up
to be paid off. And no money left in the business or
the bank.

God, oh God … the thought froze her. She had a
boy in college and a girl still in school. How on earth
was she supposed to keep them all on her salary
from the hospital? How?

'Ease off the throttle and indicate left … Mrs
Lessing, indicate left … *Left*! You're not giving
yourself enough time to —'

Maureen slammed on the breaks in an
emergency stop. 'I'm sorry. I have to go.' She pushed
open the door of the car and got out. 'I'm sorry.'

The shaken instructor, completely dumb-
founded, sat in his seat staring after her as she
dodged through the traffic and disappeared.

Hans Reiner's office was in a once imposing but now shabby apartment building in Aulstradt. After fleeing from her driving lesson, Maureen had called the accountant from a phone kiosk and arranged an urgent meeting. Now she stood outside the main entrance grim-faced, a carrier-bag full of bills in her hand. She rang the entry-phone buzzer for the tenth time but still no reply. It was unusual. Germans were always so meticulous about time-keeping and appointments.

'Maureen ...'

She turned to see Hans rushing across the road, carrying two supermarket bags full of food. He looked guilty and apologetic and his voice was slightly breathless. 'Maureen, I'm sorry to keep you waiting. I thought I had time to get some groceries.'

He shuffled around her and opened the door to the building. 'Friday afternoon, you know. It's when I usually do my weekly shopping ...'

Maureen followed him, barely listening.

'There is a very good delicatessen around the corner ... very good cheese. I hope you haven't been here long.'

'Hans, I don't understand these bills.' Maureen held up the bag in her hand. 'All bills, nothing but bills.'

'I see.' Hans attempted to summon the lift but his hand was weighed down with shopping. 'Of course, of course ... we'll talk upstairs.'

Maureen pressed the lift button, looking upwards

apprehensively as the old lift creaked and grinded its way down.

When the door opened they had to cram inside. The small lift didn't spare much room for a big man with two shopping bags, as well as Maureen and her bag.

'Hans, some of the bills go back months, years even. Oh Jesus …' Her voice tailed away as the lift ascended, creaking noisily under their weight.

'I mean, I don't understand,' she continued when the lift stopped and they had squeezed out. 'You're his accountant, for God's sake. He must have said something to you?'

'No, not really. I knew things weren't going very well of late, but …' Hans struggled with bags and keys to unlock the door to his office/apartment.

'You knew? Then why didn't you tell me?'

'But Maureen, it's against professional etiquette. James was my client.'

'Etiquette? For God's sake, Hans, you're supposed to be a friend.'

'I am. Of course I am. Come in.'

Maureen walked in and stood looking around the chaotic mess that was Hans's office. A clutter of fishing tackle and rods in the corner; piles of files and papers littering the shelves, his desk barely visible beneath more papers.

Hans saw her expression and gave another apologetic look, then bustled around trying to clear a chair for her to sit on. 'Well, the first thing for us to do is find out the size of the problem. You leave the papers with me. I'll sort everything out, get it all in order and then — you mustn't worry, Maureen. You know everything will be all right.'

Maureen's expression was bleak. 'No, I don't know that, Hans.'

Later that night, the earnest young German priest who had performed the funeral Mass called round to see the family.

Brian was out with his girlfriend, so only Maureen and Maeve sat talking with him. He asked earnest questions about the family because, although he did not say it, he had never seen either of these two females in church before the funeral.

'It's funny,' he said to Maeve, 'I could have sworn someone told me you were doing computer business studies.'

'That's my brother,' Maeve explained. 'He's at Heinrich Heine.'

'Maeve is at the International School in Düsseldorf,' Maureen said, feeling tired and emotionally drained and really wishing the priest had not come tonight. But she endeavoured to put a pleasant and brave face on it, making him coffee which he accepted gratefully, and then offering him schnapps which he refused.

'Well,' the priest said, standing up, 'I just want

you to know that everyone at St Peter's ... we are here if you need us.'

'Thank you.' Maureen escorted him to the door.

He paused at the open door and regarded her with concern. 'I realise how hard this time must be for you. But you know that God is always there, waiting to help you.'

Maureen sighed. 'I'm afraid any faith I had is rather battered at the moment.'

'That's understandable,' the priest replied softly. 'Faith is a daily battle, it has to be. I suppose the only comfort is that God must surely understand that too.'

The bedroom was warm and dark, lit only by the red glow of the bedside clock that showed *11:16.*

Maeve snuggled up close to Maureen. It was something she had done every night since the news of her father's death — abandoned her own room at night to sleep with Maureen — as if desperately needing the warm solidity of her mother's body.

The young priest had not comforted Maeve, in fact quite the opposite. 'He really annoyed me, Mum,' she whispered angrily. 'All that crap about life being like a beach.' She mimicked his voice. 'Sometimes the tide washes up a lot of debris, sometimes the sand is very clean.'

'He's just trying to do his job, Maeve.'

'Yeah, well I don't believe in God or any of it anyway.'

'A lot of people do.'

'You don't.'

'That doesn't mean I'm right. I could be wrong.'

In the long silence that followed, Maureen realised she had been wrong about a lot of things.

The phone started to ring downstairs. Maureen tried to ignore it. 'Your father believed … In fact, he started going to Mass a lot more frequently these past few years.'

'Yeah, and look where it got him,' Maeve replied bitterly. 'Smashed up on the autobahn. I mean, why him? What he had done wrong?'

The phone was still ringing. Maureen sat up. 'I'd better go and answer that.'

She padded over to the door, wondering irritably why James had taken out the extension five years ago and from then on refused to have a telephone in the bedroom.

She felt even more irritated when she descended the stairs into the hall, a second after the ringing stopped.

'Too late again,' she muttered in a jaded tone. 'Too bloody late.'

Maureen returned to Hans Reiner's apartment three days later.

The office was conspicuously tidier. Papers had

been stacked into neat piles on a table beside the desk. Accounts books had been locked away in filing cabinets.

Hans even produced a new china cup and saucer for her coffee, along with another of his apologetic looks. 'Lately, you know, these last few years,' he said, 'I have been taking on less business and doing more fishing.'

'And have you been fishing through all those bills I left here?'

Hans nodded. 'I have, yes.'

Five minutes later Maureen was poring over the documents laid out on the desk as Hans explained what he had found.

'Yes, things were tight, I knew that. But there was nothing to suggest the business was in serious trouble. It doesn't make sense. You can see ... ' he pointed, 'income down a little on last year but nothing too bad. The real problem was that James was spending more and more money and then borrowing to cover it. Look at the withdrawals — all cash. But what was he spending it on?'

Maureen didn't know, shaking her head, unable to make sense of it.

'For example,' Hans continued, 'these trips to Ireland.' He pointed to a page of figures. 'He was flying to Dublin once a month, but there are no other receipts or payments — just cash withdrawals. Did he have much business there?'

Maureen thought about it. 'I think he was

supplying software to some textile companies over there. I'm not really sure.'

'Okay. Never mind.' Hans straightened and looked at her. 'Unfortunately, there is a more immediate problem.'

Maureen knew what it was. 'The creditors?'

'No, not the creditors. I have already started to wind up the company. That shouldn't be a problem now. But do you remember when James started out on his own, he had to borrow money from the bank?' He handed her a document. 'You signed as co-guarantor for the loan.'

Maureen nodded. 'James said it was just a technicality to release the money. The house was in both our names.'

'Yes, he used the house as collateral, to guarantee the loan … so now the bank has a legal claim against your house.'

Maureen sat staring at him with horror as she realised what that meant. Hans felt he had to be blunt. 'You could lose your house now.'

'What …?' Maureen felt as if the ground was collapsing beneath her, like a sudden earthquake. To have suddenly lost James and his computer business was bad enough. But now …

'It's not my house,' Maureen blurted, 'it's my *home*. It's my children's *home*. And where are we to live if we lose our home?'

Hans could only comfort her with another of his apologetic looks. 'I'm sorry, very sorry.'

'God, what a mess,' Andrea murmured.

She and Maureen were taking a lunchtime walk through the park. Andrea could not believe what Maureen had told her.

'He got over-stretched,' Maureen explained. 'Then he started robbing Peter to pay Paul. Using different credit cards. Paying off one debt with another.'

'But you say he always paid the mortgage?'

'Yes, and the household bills. He was obviously trying to hide it. Hoping it would go away.'

'But that's madness. You were bound to find out in the end.'

'I know.' Maureen gave a bitter smile. 'Twenty-two years of marriage and you think you know someone ... God, I'm so angry I want to scream.'

'He must have been desperate.'

'But why couldn't he *say* something. Tell me. Warn me.'

'Perhaps he felt ashamed.'

'So do I,' Maureen said. 'I feel ashamed because I should have known. I should have been *told*. I mean what was James thinking of? That house was *mine* as well as his. If he knew there was a danger of us losing it, he should have faced it and warned me.'

She stopped and faced Andrea, filled with foreboding. 'How am I going to tell Brian and Maeve?'

43

A descending evening sun could still be seen in the sky, but the downstairs curtains were tightly closed.

Maeve was snuggled up on the sofa beside Eva, Brian's girlfriend, both glued to a movie on the television, nibbling from a bowl of dry cereal. Maureen had left them a pre-dinner snack of cheese sandwiches but they preferred the Special K.

Both girls were on a diet.

Maeve had always liked Eva, and still often wondered why Eva had stuck with Brian for so long. After all, as much as she fundamentally loved her brother, he was still an absolute ass. So full of himself, and infuriatingly condescending into the bargain.

But Eva was *so cool*. She was nineteen, very intelligent, a graphic art student, and she had cropped dyed blonde hair and wore Doc Martens with her mini-skirts.

Brian walked into the room eating a cheese sandwich. 'Where's Mum?'

Maeve's eyes were glued to the TV. 'Said she'd be late, she's got an appointment.'

'Not another bloody driving lesson?' Brian exclaimed. 'She's always bottled out of learning to drive before, so why learn now — when we have no car! The Audi's a write-off.'

Eva looked at him coolly. 'Give your mother a break, Brian. She's got to do something. It's her way of coping.'

'Yeah, I know, it's therapy.' Brian softened his

tone, not keen to upset Eva, but she had taken his sister and mother's side a few times lately and he was beginning to feel outnumbered.

'Yeah, right, therapy,' he repeated superciliously. 'But now, if you two could just drag yourselves away from the telly, there's some "therapeutic" washing-up that needs doing in the kitchen.'

Eva raised a glare to him — affronted by his patronising tone — and delivered her reply in German. 'Screw you. Do it yourself.'

She stood up and walked out, leaving Brian wide-eyed and flummoxed. 'Eva … What? What did I say wrong now?'

As soon as Brian had run out of the room after Eva, Maeve giggled and lay back on the sofa, turning up the sound on the TV.


On Monday afternoon, Maureen finally faced the man she had been dreading meeting again.

She had not seen him for seven years, but he didn't look a day older. Not even a sign of an extra line of worry or stress on his face, not like all the lines James had collected on his face in seven years … The difference between those men who collected piles of interest on borrowed money, and those who continually struggled to pay it, Maureen supposed.

Hans Reiner sat next to her, opposite the bank manager who studiously avoided any eye contact with Maureen, directing all his words to the accountant.

'I'm sorry, Mr Reiner, my hands are tied. Mrs Lessing clearly has a legal responsibility.'

'I would challenge that,' Hans replied.

The bank manager shrugged. 'That might delay things, but the outcome would be the same in the end. And you know it would, Mr Reiner.'

Maureen cut impatiently across their haggling, fed up with being ignored. 'Look, I accept I signed as guarantor!'

Both men looked at her.

'Legally, I owe people money, I accept that,' she continued more calmly. 'But what I want to know is — how I can pay off the debts and still keep my home?'

In the tight silence that followed, she looked from one man to the other, but neither offered her a reply.

Finally, it was not Hans Reiner but the bank manager who gave her an apologetic look, echoing the same doom-laden words, 'I'm sorry, very sorry ...'

# FOUR

Brian Lessing was a young man who spent much of his time observing the world with a cynical eye, thinking he had it all taped.

He had all the confidence of a good education and a deep pride in his English heritage. He had been born in the same city as his father and grandfather, London. The capital of culture. He remembered it well, although he had been living in Germany since the week after his ninth birthday. He spoke fluent German and was preparing to take his place in the powerful computerised world of a new dynamic Europe.

Respectability and comfort had enveloped every aspect of his life from as far back as he could remember. Thanks to his father. As a young man his father had looked into the future, recognised the speed and growth of the technological age and had made sure he was a part of it, schooling himself in all the skills of hi-tech computers while his associates were still trying to extract some kind of sensible instructions from their PC manuals. The German firm of Ericssons had recognised his capabilities and suggested he join them, offering a higher salary than the norm in England. His father had loved Ericssons, enjoyed every minute of the comfortable lifestyle their salary had provided, but had finally decided to fly his own kite and open his own business.

A business that Brian had known he would one day take over, develop and expand. Perhaps it was a matter of geography, and the closeness he felt to his friends and to his immediate surroundings; but as proud as Brian was of his English heritage, he truly believed the financial future belonged to Germany.

The dining-room table was nicely laid with fresh flowers, linen napkins, and a bottle of wine. Maureen placed a dish of lasagne and a salad bowl on the table.

Brian lifted the bottle and uncorked the wine. 'You should have told me you were going the whole hog, Mum,' he said with a grin. 'I'd have worn a shirt and tie.'

Maeve tutted sarcastically. 'Lasagne and a bottle of Peisporter is hardly going the whole hog, Brian.'

Maureen clipped her ear. 'I didn't see you helping.'

'Hey — I was doing my homework!'

'You were doing your toe nails! And you left nail polish all over the bath.'

Brian poured wine into the three glasses; then held up his own glass in a solemn toast.

'To Dad.'

'To Dad,' echoed Maeve.

Maureen looked at both of their faces and dreaded having to tell them. They still saw their father as the best dad in the whole world. A man with no faults, no weaknesses, no uncertainties. She joined in the toast with a sip of wine and quickly sat down.

'I just thought it would be good for us to get together as a family for a change, just the three of us ...' She glanced at Brian. 'That's why I didn't invite Eva.'

Maeve smirked. 'He's not seeing her anyway. They've fallen out.'

Brian gave his sister a smile of infinite patience and turned to Maureen, handing her a plate. 'Everything's fine between me and Eva.'

'Good, I'm glad you have no other problems, Brian, because I wanted to ask you and Maeve your opinion about something ... I'm thinking of selling the house.'

'What?' Maeve spluttered her wine. 'Don't be stupid, Mum! We live here.'

'Yes, but things have changed now,' Maureen said. 'And for a start, this house is going to be too big now for just you and me, Maeve.'

'Hold on,' Brian said curiously. 'Aren't we forgetting someone?'

'Oh come on, Brian, you're hardly ever here,' Maureen replied quickly. 'Besides it makes financial sense.'

'Mum,' said Brian patiently, an all-knowing look in his eyes. 'You can't run away from it, you know. Dad's death. Wherever you are, it will still hurt. But wanting to run away won't help.'

Maureen put down her knife and fork. The young fool thought he was so clever, but he had got it all wrong.

'This is our home,' Brian continued patiently. 'You can't just decide to sell it. Dad worked too hard for it.'

'Your dad got into debt,' Maureen interrupted. 'He owed money everywhere.'

'Debt?' Maeve put down the salad bowl. 'What are you talking about? Dad had loads of money.'

Maureen momentarily closed her eyes; this was turning out harder than she had anticipated. But now she had started, she decided to tell them the full truth.

'I've been speaking with Hans. I'm afraid we've had to put the computer business into liquidation.'

'That's ridiculous!' Brian was still stunned. 'What the hell made you do that! The business was doing great.'

'No, it wasn't doing great, Brian. It was weighed down with unpaid bills.'

'Says who?' Brian's anger was flaring. 'Dad worked his back off setting up that company. You can't just sell off everything he built!'

'Brian, it's all gone. There's nothing left for us. It's all owed to the bank. Even the house.'

Brian wasn't prepared to hear anymore, refusing to believe his father had left them in a financial mess. He shoved back his chair and stood up. 'I don't believe you. You've got it all wrong. You're panicking and you're wrong. I'll talk to Hans Reiner myself tomorrow.'

Maureen quickly followed him into the kitchen, Maeve at her elbow. 'Brian, I found drawers full of unpaid bills in his study.'

'So? Are you saying he was hiding them?'

'I don't know. Maybe he just didn't want to worry us. Your father was a proud man. I think he felt ashamed.'

'Ashamed?' Brian stepped back as if she had spit at him, revolted by any criticism of his father. 'I don't want to hear any more of this.'

Maureen grabbed his arm, desperate to make him understand. 'Now you listen to me! We may have nothing now, but we're still a family and we're still here! It's us three now. Just the three of us. And somehow we have to cope. I don't know why the business got so messed up. I'm as confused as you are, Brian. But we've got to see this thing through together. Do you hear me ... *together*.'

Brian's angry eyes seemed to be sucking her in, his furious face determined. 'I won't let them take the house,' he said. 'I won't.'

And how the hell will a college boy like you, without even a job or a penny to your name, manage to stop them? Maureen thought wearily.

Maeve did not sleep with her mother that night. She locked herself away in her room, refusing to answer any knocks.

Maureen went to her own bed feeling very upset: both children seemed to be blaming her for everything that had gone wrong, as if she personally had caused their father's death, ruined his business … God Almighty.

Maureen knew she was facing another sleepless night.

Half an hour later she was propped up in bed sifting through a pile of James's business letters, searching for some kind of clue as to what had happened, what had caused the business to go so terribly wrong.

She picked up a wad of Visa bills and read through them … Aer Lingus … Aer Lingus … What business had he in Ireland? She checked through the listed calls on the telephone bills. None to Ireland.

She took off her reading glasses and stared up at the ceiling, wondering at the mystery of it. Why would a man fly regularly by Aer Lingus to Ireland, yet leave no other trace of his visits there?

She eventually slept for about three hours, rising at six and ready for work by seven, having decided she might as well go in early and make herself useful. If nothing else, it would distract her mind from her own problems.

The post arrived as she was putting on her coat. She groaned when she lifted it from the hall floor and saw what the postman had delivered — more bills! She flicked through them. Access. Rates. Vodafone.'

She was about to throw the bills onto the hall table, then stopped — Vodafone?

Amongst all the bills she had searched through, there had not been one bill from Vodafone. Yet James had been using his mobile for years.

She ripped open the envelope and scanned down the list of calls — dozens of them — all to the same number ... a number in Ireland.

An uneasy feeling began to stir in the pit of her stomach. She walked quickly back down the hallway and straight into James's study. His mobile phone was on the desk, where she had left it.

She sat down at the desk and spread the Vodafone bill in front of her. She picked up the mobile, hesitated for a moment, then took a deep breath and tapped in the Irish telephone number ... it started to ring.

She glanced at her watch; it was only 7.05, so if it was a business number there would be no reply.

The ringing stopped, a voice answered 'Hello'.

Maureen's confusion was total ... the voice at the other end was that of a young boy ... a very young boy of about five or six years old.

'Hello ...' the boy repeated. His accent was very Irish.

'Yes, em, hello,' Maureen stuttered. 'I was trying to contact a Mr James Lessing?'

'Daddy is away working,' the boy said. 'But he'll be coming home soon.'

Maureen shrank back on the chair in horror, sure she must have made some kind of terrible mistake.

'Is … is your daddy's name James Lessing?'

'Yeah, and so is mine,' the boy said proudly.

'And … and where is your daddy away working? Do you know?'

'Course I know. He's away working in Germany. That's where he always goes to work. But he'll be coming home soon … Do you want to speak to Mammy? She's still asleep.'

Maureen's finger fumbled for the cut-off button, her face white and stricken. She sat for a long time in the silence, paralysed, listening to the thudding sound of her own heart.

# FIVE

Inside the aircraft the overhead lights flashed on: *No Smoking. Fasten Seat Belts.*

Maeve was flicking through the Duty Free magazine. 'Brian'll be in seventh heaven having the house all to himself,' she said. 'He'll be able to bring Eva in every night to sleep with him. And no worries about getting caught.'

Maureen was not listening, her gaze fixed on the window. It was eight years since she had last come home to Ireland. Eight long years …

The captain's voice crackled overhead. '*Ladies and Gentlemen, we are now approaching the coastline of Ireland. The temperature in Dublin is a balmy seventy degrees …*'

Maureen stared down as the coastline became visible in the clear sunlight, seeming to stretch away into infinity. And then the land, rich and green and verdant …

Then it came — the landing; so smooth that only a slight bump revealed that the wheels had touched the ground.

A stewardess spoke through the Tannoy. '*Ladies and Gentlemen, welcome to Dublin. Thank you for flying with Aer Lingus. We hope that you have enjoyed your flight, and that we will see you on board again soon.*'

She then repeated the whole thing in Gaelic.

Now they had arrived, Maureen felt a sudden rush of fear, dreading what she might find here in Ireland.

'Mum, are you okay?'

Maureen took a calming breath and smiled at Maeve. 'I'm fine, love. You know how much I hate take-off and landing. But listen,' she added quickly, 'when we see Nora and Sean, just remember, we're here for a break, that's all. A nice, relaxing break.'

Maeve was looking at her oddly. 'I know that. Why else would we come to Ireland?'

Maureen forced a grin. 'Ah, you know what I mean. I just want no fuss.'

Nora and Sean Mullen stood waiting in the noise and bustle of the airport terminal.

Even Auntie Bridget had travelled out with Sean and Nora to welcome Maureen home. They stood scanning the lines of passengers as the terminal became packed with boisterous groups, welcoming friends and relatives.

Bridget saw them first. 'That's them!' She waved furiously, '*Maureen*! *Maeve*!' She slapped her son's arm. 'Sean, wave will you. *Maureen*!'

A minute later Maureen and Maeve found themselves enveloped into the clamour and welcoming arms of the Mullens.

Relief flooded over Maureen as she was hugged

tightly by Nora. *Oh God, the warm hugging arms of a friend. Was there anything better?*

Nora drew back her head and gazed tearfully at Maureen, her childhood and lifelong friend, thinking she understood the reason for this visit — Maureen had come back to Ireland to try and ease the heartache of James's death.

'Welcome home, Maureen,' she whispered. 'Don't worry, we'll look after you.'

The drive from the airport was in Sean's Espace taxi van. Maureen couldn't get over the increase of traffic on the Dublin roads.

'Ah well, we're a Celtic Tiger now,' Sean said. 'So it's the rush hour twenty-four hours of the bleedin' day —' He blasted his horn. 'Get on you dozy oul fart!' Maureen stared through the window as Sean gave his own running commentary of the ills of his taxi driving life …

'Sean!' his mother shouted. 'Language!'

'It's true but.'

'I don't care if it's true, mind your language in front of Maeve!'

Maeve giggled.

'Now you see that, Maureen?' Sean continued. 'Now that's a prime example. They're after putting in these bus and taxi lanes and some gobshite has parked right slap-bang in the middle.' He pulled out, and a horn blared.

Nora slipped her arm inside Maureen's. 'Don't mind him. If he was a bit smarter he'd be stressed. As it is he's just annoyed. How long can you stay?'

'Not long, Nora. It's difficult, what with work and Maeve's school ...' Maureen was still gazing in amazement through the window. 'God what a change. The whole place is completely different.'

Nora laughed. 'Tell me about it. We've got bookings up to November.'

Maureen turned to her. 'Are you sure you can fit us in?'

'Fit you in?' Auntie Bridget interrupted. 'Maureen, you're family. Of course we can fit you in. We just cancelled a couple of tourists, that's all.'

'Bridget — you shouldn't have. The tourists are your business.'

'Ah feck em,' Bridget grinned. 'When did tourists ever come before family.'

'Mother!' Sean shouted. 'Language!'

'And anyway,' Bridget continued more seriously. 'There's loads of other places they can go to. We booked them into a nice place further down the road instead.'

The Espace drew up outside the Mullen's B&B hotel, one of a number of similar small hotels in the redeveloped Georgian terrace. It wasn't very large, only twelve bedrooms, but it was well-kept and full of eclectic charm. A profusion of flower tubs and hanging baskets decorated the front.

Maureen stood looking around her. 'God, everything's changed … everything.'

Two teenage girls came running out of the house with squeals of delight and descended down the steps. '*Maeve!*' they chorused.

Maeve dropped her bag and charged, bawling out joyously, '*Niamh! Jenny!*'

A moment later Maeve was wrapped inside the four arms of the Mullen's two young daughters and all three of them were talking at once.

'Jesus, now I know why Brian never comes here,' Sean grinned, lifting out Maureen's bags. 'Come on, Maureen, in you get for a nice cup of Ma's tea.'

Maureen didn't have to be told twice. 'A nice cup of tea — there's nothing I'd like more.'


A large conservatory had been built onto the back of the Georgian house to serve as a private dining/family room for the Mullens. It was well-equipped, nicely furnished, and a door led through to the hotel's kitchen for easy access.

Maureen and Maeve sat with the family around a large centre table laden with the remains of a banquet supper. Maureen had never eaten so much food, nor so good.

'Yeah,' Sean said, 'there's been a lot of development of the old area and that's a fact.'

Maureen replied musingly, 'And this place. Just look at it …' Through the lace curtains on the opposite window she could just see the pretty dining room already laid out for tomorrow's breakfast. 'It's just lovely now. Really grand. But what made you decide to turn it into a hotel?'

Sean was pleased at her approval. 'Well, it made sense, especially after Da had died.'

'Without that booming laughter and loud lovely singing voice of his,' Bridget cut in, 'this place was like a mausoleum, as quiet as a morgue. So we decided to bring some noise and laughter and life back into it, some people. So we had it all refurbished and opened it as a hotel.'

Sean continued answering Maureen's question as if his mother hadn't spoken. 'So we thought, why don't we make the place pay for itself. Make it self-sufficient like.'

Nora nodded. 'It's a three-way partnership. I run the front of the house and Bridget is in charge of the kitchen. It made the best sense, with me being so alluring and glamorous, and Bridget being such a good cook.'

Nora's two daughters laughed with their mother. Bridget was not so amused. 'What's with the good — only yesterday you were saying I was a *great* cook.'

'And so you are, but I don't want your head to get too big,' Nora replied, winking at Maureen. 'The girls help out with rooms. And Sean does the garden in between his taxi runs.'

'And bloody useless he is too,' Bridget opined.

Sean grinned. 'Ah, but I'm cheap.'

The three teenage girls were bored with the conversation of the parents. Niamh nudged Maeve. 'You want to come to my room, check out my new CD's?'

'Yeah, great.' Maeve jumped to her feet.

'I've got Boyzone's new CD. Are they still big in Germany?'

'Mega!'

Maureen watched her daughter leave the room at speed with the two Mullen girls, pleased to see Maeve looking happy again, but her worry about Brian brought an anxious expression to her eyes.

Nora noticed it. 'What's up, Maureen? They're only going up to play a bit of music. Boyzone non-stop no doubt.'

Maureen tried to smile. 'No, it's not that … I was just wondering how Brian is coping on his own back in Germany.'

Brian was in his father's study, searching through the papers and files looking for his own clues to what had gone wrong with the business.

He had been searching for hours — nothing. He had read through everything carefully, and ascertained that the company had been doing fairly well. Enough business and money coming in. So why all the unpaid bills? And why did some of them date back so far — the accruing interest alone was economic insanity. He couldn't believe his father had deliberately been so stupid.

The sudden ringing of the door bell jolted him. He quickly put the papers back in the drawers and left the study, switching off the light and closing the door behind him.

When he opened the front door, Eva was standing there holding up a bottle of wine.

'Surprise!' she smiled.

The table had been cleared, the washing-up had been done, and Bridget had gone to bed to get a good night's sleep in readiness for the early breakfasts she would have to cook for the tourists in the morning.

Maureen and Nora sat alone at the table, each holding a mug of freshly-percolated coffee. Nora added a tot of whiskey into each mug.

'No, stop, Nora, I shouldn't'

'It's just a tiny tot,' Nora grinned. She lifted her mug in a toast. To old times. *Slainte.*'

'Old times,' Maureen agreed, but could not smile. She was desperate to unburden herself to Nora, desperate to share her confusion and grief.

'You look tired,' Nora said softly. 'Is it tough going for you?'

'Yes ...' Maureen decided to tell her. 'We could lose the house, Nora. Everything. I didn't know it, but James ... well, James had serious money problems.'

Nora was shocked. 'Lose the house? God, Maureen ...' Then suddenly realising. 'Is that why you came home?'

'Yes.'

Maureen wanted to tell Nora the truth, about her *real* reason for coming to Ireland, but she couldn't. She suddenly saw herself as others might see her: the classic old cliché of the middle-aged wife, lied to by her husband for years and never suspecting a thing, never once realising that she was being taken for a fool ... Just the thought of it made her go cold with embarrassment.

'It's his business, you see. It's all very complicated ...' Maureen's voice trailed off.

Nora thought she understood, and didn't want to pry too much. 'I understand,' she said softly. 'And you don't want anyone to know?'

'No. It's my pride, I suppose. I mean, it feels odd, Nora. Me coming back home and seeing all these changes. The success you've made of your lives, and me with all my financial troubles ... I'm embarrassed.'

'Don't be.' Nora insisted. 'Now listen, if you want help, just ask for help. And you know Sean and Bridget will do anything for you. All you have to do is say the word. Until then I don't know anything, right?'

Maureen was touched. 'Thanks, Nora.'

'And don't you worry about Maeve. The girls will look after her. They always love having her here.'

In Monchengladbach, Brian grinned as he led a reluctant Eva into his mother's bedroom.

'Oh come on, it's the only double bed in the house. Do you want to stay or not?'

'Yes, but not in your mum's room.'

Brian laughed. He had drank half her bottle of wine, and opened a second. He felt devil-may-care and thought Eva looked beautiful. But then, Eva always did.

'It's just a bed, Eva,' he said. 'And it's not exactly a mortal sin is it?'

Eva was smiling, half-tempted, half-reluctant. 'I don't think your mother would like it.'

'Maybe she wouldn't, but *I* would.' He grinned and grabbed her.

The lights were still on when Maureen entered her room. Maeve was fast asleep in one of the twin beds, a Boyzone disc still blaring out from her headphones.

Maureen stood staring down at Maeve for a long moment, thinking how very young her daughter still looked when she was asleep, not like a maturing girl at all, but childlike, sweet and innocent and vulnerable.

She bent down and turned off the Discman, gently removed the headphones, and kissed her daughter's cheek. 'Night, love.'

Maureen turned to close the curtains, then hesitated. She stood for a time staring out the dark window at the lights of Dublin.

The small voice that had been echoing continually inside her head, nearly driving her crazy, welled up again, *'Daddy's away working … Daddy's away …'*

# SIX

When Maeve, Niamh and Jenny reached the Cyber Café the place was busy and noisy with young tourists and locals, all clamouring for service.

The girls decided to drink their cappuccinos outside in the sunlight. Banks of VDU screens flickered away behind them. At the other side of the road a photographer and his assistant were setting up a camera for a fashion shoot, using the Cyber Café as the dramatic backdrop.

'Wow. Neat place.' Maeve giggled. 'Is it always this busy?'

'Yeah.' Niamh nodded, 'This place is buzzin'. Weekends especially. It's mad in Dublin these days. Stag parties from England, everything.'

Three young lads wearing red Manchester United shirts sauntered over, eyeing the girls as they sat themselves down at a nearby table.

Jenny grinned over her coffee. 'Fancy your chances, lads?' She lowered her voice as Niamh and Maeve laughed. 'We can do better!'

She suddenly challenged Maeve. 'Speaking of which, why didn't your hunky brother come over with you?'

Brian's beaten-up old Volkswagen was parked outside his father's business, now bereft of employees and all assets, including the furniture. Hans Reiner was inside, making a note of the few pieces of equipment that were left — a few computers, a couple of telephones and a fax machine stacked by the door.

Brian was becoming frustrated at Hans Reiner's hard-headedness.

'Look, I'm his son, and this was his business. So I'm entitled to know what has been going on.'

Hans Reiner continued writing his notes. 'You want to know what has been going on? Of course you do. But you must talk to your mother. It's not for me to say.'

'Oh, that's shit and you know it, Hans. She's all over the place. I hear her crying herself to sleep at night. She even started taking driving lessons, for heaven's sake! Fucking driving lessons — at her age? She needs my *help*. So don't say it's up to her.'

Hans was sympathetic but firm. 'I'm sorry, Brian. I'm just doing an inventory of what's left of the stock and equipment.'

'You know she's gone off to Ireland, don't you? To speak to the creditors. Was that your idea?'

Hans surprise was evident, followed by his puzzlement. 'No … You must be mistaken. There are no creditors in Ireland.'

'What?' Brian's brow creased with confusion. 'No creditors in Ireland?'

'No, none at all.' Hans frowned. 'I didn't even know she had gone to Ireland.'

Uncertain of which way to go next, Maureen walked along the seafront road in Bray, below the towering landscape of mountains. She approached a Garda officer standing outside an amusement arcade, wanting to ask directions. Hesitating, she decided against it and turned back towards Bray's town centre.

A kind and helpful telephonist in Directory Enquiries had responded to her plea for help and given her the address of the Irish telephone number.

Five minutes later, in Bray's Centre, she approached a young man who looked at the paper in her hand, read the address, and pointed her in the direction of Wicklow.

'It's not far,' he told her. 'It'll only take you about fifteen minutes to walk it. Straight on to the roundabout, then the third turning to your right.'

Maureen finally reached her destination. A nice road with a row of bungalows and neatly-kept front gardens, and kids bicycling on the pavements.

She walked along slowly, her eyes searching, but couldn't find the number of the house: most of the bungalows seemed to have names.

A football suddenly sailed over a hedge, hitting her shoulder and dropping at her feet. A child's voice cried out. 'Mam … Mam, my ball.'

Maureen smiled, picked up the ball and walked to the nearby gate, calling 'Hello. Hello? It's here. Your football is here … Hello …'

A small boy appeared from the side of the front garden at the gate. 'That's my ball. I'm playing football.'

Maureen froze as she stared at him. The boy was the image of James … a smaller version of James, the same smile, the same chestnut red hair … and the voice was familiar. This must be the house.

The boy was reaching upwards. 'My ball. Can I have my ball back?'

Maureen couldn't speak. Her legs felt like jelly. Her voice, when she finally spoke seemed to belong to someone else.

'What's your name?'

'Jamie.'

The name was like a knife in her heart.

'How old are you?'

'Five.'

The knife went deeper into Maureen's heart as she realised the implication. *Five.* So it must have been going on for years.

From somewhere near the back of the house Maureen suddenly heard a woman's voice — 'Jamie? Where are you? What are you doing …?'

Maureen looked up, stunned. The woman had a *German* accent!

And then Maureen caught sight of her, although

the woman was so busy looking round the bushes for her son, she did not see Maureen. An attractive woman in her thirties, fashionably dressed in a long peasant skirt and designer sweater.

Maureen quickly shoved the ball into the boy's arms and rushed away, faster and faster ... *Jamie — James.*

A woman in her *thirties* for Christ's sake! How bloody typical! A woman almost twenty years younger than his wife! Faster, faster ... *Jamie — James.* Maureen was beginning to find it difficult to catch her breath.

She began to run, desperate to get away. *Faster.*

Finally she slowed down, out of sight of the bungalow, looking around but seeing nothing. Lost in a world of her own that was turning into a pain-filled nightmare.

# SEVEN

No one in the family would believe her, she knew that. She could hardly believe it herself. She needed evidence, if only to prove the awful truth to herself.

In a Bray camera shop, she made her purchase, using the opportunity to ask the young sales assistant some seemingly innocent questions about the area. She discovered that the nearest Primary School to the bungalow was St Mary's.

The following morning she rose very early and was on the bus out to Bray in good time, standing across the road from St Mary's school, having taken up a keen vantage point behind a tree.

She really would have preferred to stand in the telephone kiosk a few yards up the road, but had decided it was not the best place from which to try and take photographs, the glass being too grimy and polluted.

She peered over at the school. Some of the kids were playing in the front yard prior to Assembly. Jamie was not amongst them.

He arrived a few minutes later in car driven by the German woman. Maureen watched her. Today she was not wearing a long peasant skirt, but dressed in a smart suit. She took the boy's hand, walking with him through the school gate.

*Click.*

A man in his late thirties, obviously a teacher, came out of the school building and seemed to give the German woman and her boy a rather special and over-the-top welcome, grabbing Jamie around the waist and hoisting him laughingly into the air. *Click.*

A minute later the teacher blew a whistle and gestured for all the children to go inside.

The German woman leaned down and kissed Jamie goodbye.

*Click.*

Jamie ran inside.

The teacher and mother delayed for a few minutes together in private conversation which seemed somewhat animated — she looked very worried, and he seemed to be giving her words of encouragement.

*Click. Click. Click.*

He must have succeeded in cheering her, because she was smiling when she moved away and walked back to her car, *Click.* She even turned and waved to him, *Click*, before opening the door of her car, *Click*, and driving away. *Click. Click. Click.*

Maureen watched the car until it disappeared around the corner, the bile in her stomach making her feel nauseous and pathetic … Oh, it was galling … not only was the German woman so much younger then her, so much more chic in every way — the bitch could also *drive a car.*

The shame of it.

The shame of hiding behind trees and taking secret photographs began to consume Maureen even before she returned to the Mullens.

She stayed out all day, walking around aimlessly, staring at the sea, thinking of everything that had happened, and the shame of her own sneaky actions. What had she been reduced to? The fact that she was the innocent victim in all this, the one who had been duped and betrayed, didn't soothe her conscience at all.

As soon as she returned to the Mullens, she tried to wash away her shame with a very hot bath, finally lying back and putting a wet flannel over her face to block out all light and thought.

She had not heard Jamie speak directly to the German woman, so how she could be sure the woman was his mother?

She had to be.

'Mum? Mum … Are you okay?'

Maureen pulled the flannel from her face and saw Maeve standing in the bathroom staring quizzically at her.

'Are you okay?' Maeve asked again.

'Yeah, I'm fine,' Maureen answered brightly, grabbing the flannel and soaping it. 'Just got a bit of a headache.' She changed the subject. 'So, how did you get on?'

'Great — except I got my period.' Maeve sat down on the side of the bath. 'Hey, listen, d'you know why so many bands come from Ireland? It's because they don't pay any income tax. None at all. Isn't that great? I mean, it's like the government, you know, encouraging new talent.'

Maureen's expression was wry, she didn't think it was fair. 'Well, that's one way of looking at it.'

'So what news with the creditors?' Maeve asked.

'What? Oh, er … none.'

'None? But they must have said something. I mean —'

'Maeve, I'm tired, alright?' Maureen squeezed out the flannel. 'I've had a long day and I've got a splitting headache.'

'Shall I ask Nora for a couple of aspirins for you?'

'No! Just let me lie down for a bit. And tell Nora not to bother with food for me. Okay?'

'Yeah, okay …' Maeve stood up, still looking concerned. 'Oh by the way, Brian rang — *again*. Said he couldn't get through on your mobile.'

'The battery's flat,' Maureen lied. She had switched her mobile off. After Maeve had left, Maureen sat in the cooling water of the bath listening to the drip … drip … drip of the tap.

The following morning she took a bus into Dublin City and left the camera film into a shop that did two-hour developing.

She wandered around the shops and returned at

the allocated time to find that photographs were not ready.

'So when?'

'Come back in an hour.'

She strolled up to Westmoreland Street and relaxed for an hour in Bewley's Coffee House, glad to get the weight off her feet, comforted by the delicious smell of the Brazilian coffee beans.

When she returned to the photographic shop the young man behind the counter smiled cheerfully. 'All ready for you. Sorry about the delay.'

In a small quayside café, she sat at a table by the plate glass window and took out the photographs from the packet … She had expected them to be foggy or slightly out of focus, she had never having been too hot with cameras, but every single shot was as clear as reality.

The German woman with Jamie … With Jamie and the teacher … Just her and the teacher … Alone, smiling as she walked to her car …

Maureen quickly shoved the photographs back into the packet, unable to look at them anymore, turning her face to the window, staring out, wondering what she was going to do now?

The waitress brought her a cup of tea. Maureen dropped in two lumps of sugar and spent minutes stirring it, staring down into the swirling hot liquid before finally looking up.

She had another couple of days to get to the very bottom of this, and that's what she would do. By fair means or foul, she would do whatever was necessary to find out the truth.

# EIGHT

The dining-room of the Mullen's hotel was filling up with guests ready for their breakfast.

Bridget was relentless at the stove while Niamh and Jenny flitted back and forth between the dining-room and kitchen carrying fresh orders and dirty plates, all three females talking at once.

'Two "fulls" for table five.'

'Coming up.'

'A single for table three, eggs only, no sausages or bacon.'

'*BOO*!' Sean Mullen jumped out from behind the kitchen door, scaring Jenny and Niamh as they came in with a pile of plates.

Jenny dropped her cutlery. 'Ah, Dad! Will you stop doing that!'

Bridget glanced at her son. 'I have your breakfast ready for you, Sean.'

'Thanks, Ma.' Sean grinned, taking off his jacket. 'With the stealth of a panther Sean Mullen removes his jacket.'

'Panser, more like, ' Niamh grunted.

'Then, with all the cool sophistication of James Bond, he sits down at the table ...' Sean sat down and lifted his knife and fork in a firm grip, like a navvy in a café, waiting to tuck in.

The front doorbell buzzed loudly. Bridget roared from the stove, 'Sean, answer the front door.'

'What? Why me?'

'The girls are busy.'

'Jesus,' Sean grumbled, standing up again. 'If I'm not working at bleedin' work, I'm working at bleedin' home.'

Bridget handed Niamh a plate. 'Here you go, love. Table six. Inspector Clouseau.'

Nora entered the kitchen, passing Sean on his way out. She stared at him. 'I thought you were coming back for your breakfast?'

'I *have* come back for my breakfast. There's someone at the front door.'

'I'll go. You sit down.' Nora called over to Bridget. 'Two full for table four, and more tea and soda bread for table two.' Nora turned away and almost bumped into Maureen. 'Oh … morning, Maureen.'

Maureen felt embarrassed as she entered the kitchen. The family usually sat down to eat at seven, before the guest breakfasts started. 'Sorry,' she said with genuine apology. 'We overslept. Maeve's still out for the count.'

Nora smiled. 'Don't worry about it.' She caught Niamh's arm. 'Get the front door will you. If it's the electrician, take him up to number ten.'

'Number ten?' said Sean. 'I thought I fixed that.'

'Ha!' Bridget turned from the stove. 'And we all know what "thought" did? Peed in his pants and thought he was sweating.' She smiled at Maureen. 'Can I get you a bit of breakfast? I have a lovely bit of bacon here, fresh mushrooms, tomatoes, nice bit of fried bread —'

'No. Thanks, Bridget, I'm fine. Besides, you're busy.'

Bridget was taking none of this. 'Rubbish! You've got to eat, girl. Sit yourself down.'

'Actually, I'm running a bit late.'

'Then you can have Sean's. He's in no hurry. C'mon, I have it here ready.' Bridget lifted over a huge plate laden with the traditional Irish "full" breakfast. 'That'll set you up for the rest of the day.'

Maureen had no appetite for anything, and the sight of Sean's face as he watched his breakfast being given to someone else was a picture.

'No, really, Bridget, I couldn't. Anyway, I have to go out. And I'm late.'

'Ah, c'mon …'

'Bridget — she's not hungry,' Nora said firmly. 'She doesn't want it.'

Bridget shook her head and turned back to the stove. Sean lifted the plate onto the mat in front of him and began tucking in before anyone changed their mind. But he didn't like to be inhospitable … 'If you just hang on there for a minute, Maureen, I'll give you a lift to wherever you're going.'

'No, no really.'

'It's no problem, just hang on.'

'Sean, she's fine, she doesn't need a lift,' Nora said firmly, then looked knowingly at Maureen, sure she was going out to a meeting with the creditors. 'So, everything okay?'

'Yes.' Maureen smiled too brightly. 'Yes, great … but, em, I might stay over a bit longer, if that's okay?'

'That's brilliant,' Nora grinned. 'More time for us to chat.'

'Well, I'll see you all later … Maureen was already out the door before Sean had time to answer her. Instinctively he sensed that something was not quite right, and that Nora knew something about Maureen that he didn't know.

He gave his wife a long quizzical stare. 'Am I missing something here?'

'Your fried tomatoes,' Bridget said, carrying over a steaming frying-pan. 'I forgot to put them on your plate.'

A few yards down the street, Maureen saw a taxi and hailed it. She really was late and the bus would be too slow to get her there on time.

She yanked open the rear door and climbed into the taxi. 'Bray,' she said to the driver. 'And can you go as fast as possible.'

The sunlight streaming through a crack in the curtains hit Maeve's face. She opened her eyes and moved, wincing at the pain in her abdomen. Rolling out of bed, she padded into the bathroom, found her tampon box, and groaned to see it empty.

She returned to the wardrobe and lifted out her mother's hold-all onto the bed. Rifling through it hurriedly she pulled out a packet of tampons from the bottom of the bag ... 'Why hide them at the bottom,' she muttered irritably, 'they're nothing to be ashamed of.'

Something caught her eye a shiny yellow-and-blue photographic envelope that looked brand new ...

Maeve was puzzled. The packet had not been there last time she'd looked for something in her mother's hold-all, only two days ago.

She took out the photographs and laid them out on the bed, staring down at each one, completely mystified.

Nearly all the photos were of a woman and a small boy ... a few of the woman with a man, probably her husband, and then — Maeve's heart missed a beat as she stared at the boy — he was the image of Dad ... the image of Brian ... shorter and smaller, but the spitting image ...

A harder, colder, more intense look came into Maeve's eyes as she stared again at the woman in the photographs.

In the corridor of St Mary's Primary School in Bray, two female teachers were leading their children in duck-file to their classrooms.

Michael Docherty, the young headmaster, emerged from the boys' toilets with his shirt-sleeves rolled up, a screwdriver and spanners in his hands — just in time to see Jamie arriving with his mother.

'Morning, Jamie. You'd better get in there, kid. Don't want to be late for register, do you?'

'No, sir. Bye, Mam.' Jamie rushed in to the classroom.

'So, how goes it, Liza?' Michael Docherty asked cheerfully, but Liza was disapprovingly eyeing Michael's dirty hands.

'You could pay someone to do that for you, you know,' she said crisply.

'I did pay someone. I'm still waiting for them to come back. Unfortunately the kids can't wait. When they've got to go, they've got to go.'

Michael grinned. 'Look, Liza, if you're worried about Jamie, don't be. The whole place has been disinfected. He'll be fine.'

Liza looked apologetic. 'Is it that obvious?'

'It is.' Michael shrugged. 'But isn't that what mother's are supposed to do? Worry. Here — I won't offer you my arm, but I'll escort you out.'

Liza smiled and fell into an easy stride beside him as they walked towards the main door. 'So, will we be having the pleasure of your company at choir practice tonight?' Michael asked.

'I don't know. I'm expecting a phone call from James. He didn't call at the weekend. To be honest, Michael, he hasn't phoned me for weeks, not since he went back to Germany. I don't understand why.'

'Oh. I see.' Michael glanced away — the subject of Liza and James Lessing was not one he liked to discuss. 'Well, I'll ring you later, okay.'

Liza hesitated. 'Michael, can I leave my car in your parking space today? I have to go into Dublin.'

'Be my guest.' Michael smiled at her. 'Leave me the keys and I'll do it for you.'


Maureen was sitting in the back of the taxi, parked a few yards up the road from the school on the opposite side.

She saw the German woman and the teacher come out of the school building into the playground, and quickly shrank down a bit in her seat, her blue eyes watching.

'Have you decided yet?' the young taxi-driver said lethargically, in a slow Dublin drawl. 'Are you getting out? Or are you thinking of staying in and going on somewhere else.'

'I'll tell you in a minute,' Maureen snapped. 'Just keep your meter running and don't worry about it.'

'Fine by me,' said the driver, taking out his cigarettes. 'Just so long as you don't mind paying. I mean, some people, you know, they expect you to sit waiting ....'

Maureen was not listening to him, his voice droning outside of her consciousness as she watched the German woman hand over some keys to the teacher; then a nod and she turned away, walking out of the School gate — not to her car, but in the opposite direction ...

Maureen started in surprise — what was going on? Her plan was to get the taxi driver to follow the woman's car, see where she went to, find out if she had a job or what, but it was the *teacher* who was getting into the woman's car, reversing it and backing it into the parking bay.

' ... and so I says to him, I says, I can't wait here forever and for nothing, time is money, especially to taxi drivers —'

'How much?' Maureen snapped.

'What?'

'I'm getting out. So how much do I owe you?'

'Let me see now, that'll be ... seventeen pounds fifty.'

'Robbery.' Maureen flung him a twenty-pound note. 'Keep the change.' She pushed open the door and hurried across the road to follow the German woman, catching sight of her on the next street.

At a wrought-iron table on the Mullen's patio, Maeve sat in grave thought, wondering about the photographs, dreading her own suspicions. No, it wasn't possible. Dad would never do anything like that …

Behind her Nora was cleaning the windows, glancing over her shoulder to look worriedly at the girl.

'Maybe we could go out later,' Nora said. 'You and me, Maeve? Meet the girls from school. Sean said he might give us a bit of a tour round when he finishes work. Would you like that?'

'Yeah, lovely …' Maeve turned and looked at her. 'Nora, did Mum say exactly where she was going?'

Nora was still convinced that Maureen had gone to a meeting with the creditors, but she wasn't sure how much Maeve knew about the financial problems. She answered noncommittally. 'No …. To see some old friends, I think.'

Maeve stood up and faced Nora with great dignity. 'It's okay, Nora. I know about Dad. You see, Mum and me, we have no secrets. So I know all about Dad.'

Nora could see she knew. She looked at Maeve sadly. 'So you know all about the creditors then?'

Sean Mullen would have been furious to know that Maureen had used another driver's taxi instead of his own. He had left the hotel only ten minutes after Maureen, and his first fare was to Bray.

In a busy Bray street, Sean had just dropped off a

businessman who had not uttered one word on the journey, not even in answer to his pleasant and polite chatter. Sean sat for a moment watching his passenger walking briskly away.

'Tip, sir? Oh no, sir, I wouldn't dream of accepting a tip, sir — you tight-arsed little bollix!'

He sat forward, about to change gears from neutral to first, and stopped, a puzzled frown on his face as he stared at a woman rushing along on the opposite side of the road … was that Maureen?

He leaned over to lower the passenger window and call out to her, but a second later she was gone.

Sean sat back, uncertain. Was it Maureen? Well, if it wasn't Maureen, it was definitely her twin.

In the Dart station, Maureen could hear the tannoy announcing the departure of the Dublin train. She hurried down the steps onto the platform, seeing the German woman step into a carriage. Maureen rushed forward and climbed onto the train, just in time.

She stood back, observing the German woman as she settled herself into a seat, noting everything about her, the well-groomed hair and make-up, the fashionable designer clothes … Was it James's money that had paid for those clothes? Money that should have gone to his family?

Maureen felt the rage and quickly looked away

from the woman, hating her. Her and her bastard son.

Back on the streets, Maureen continued to follow the woman every step of the way in Dublin ... down the narrow roads behind the Westbury Hotel, on and on past the fashionable boutiques. She watched the woman glance over the window displays of every one; finally stopping at a small but exclusive designer knitwear shop, and going inside.

Maureen stopped also, pretending great interest in the clothes in the window, her eyes fixed on a classy maroon suit of fine Irish wool, topped by a beautiful maroon and blue beret ... The cream price-card positioned by the feet of the plastic mannequin had small and discreet black numbers on it, £1150.

Holy God! In Germany you could buy a reasonable second-hand car for that.

She slowly raised her eyes and saw the German woman inside, laughing and chatting with the trendy young sales staff as she examined a rack of expensive-looking sweaters.

Maureen watched her grimly, the cost of the sweaters was clearly no problem for her. She obviously had no idea that her constant supply of money had crashed.

In Düsseldorf, Brian had done his best to throw off his 'student' image and look the part; freshly shaved for once, and wearing his father's jacket and tie over his jeans, hoping to reassure the bank manager that he could be relied upon.

But the bank manager was neither amenable nor open to persuasion. He stated the facts to Brian concisely.

'Sixty days?' Brian was seething. 'But that's only two months! We can do nothing in two months. And we're not going anywhere in two months either!'

The manager clearly did not like his attitude. 'I think you'll find your mother understands the situation better than you do. Unless the debts are met, the house will have to be sold,' he said tersely, rising to his feet. 'Now if you will excuse me, I have another appointment.'

Brian stood up and glared at the man, his hands and jaw clenching with humiliation and fury. Finally he spoke, '*You little fuck,*' he hissed. 'Right now all my mother understands is that we are losing our home!'

*Jesus, what was she doing now? What business had she here?* Maureen had followed the German woman into the reception area of a hospital …

Maureen hesitated, watching her as she stood with a couple of nurses and visitors waiting for one of the lifts. Maureen slowly ambled up to join them. *Was she visiting someone here?*

One of the visitors stood with a young boy of about thirteen years old who seemed to be bald under his baseball cap. She spoke to the German woman in a friendly tone. 'Are you at clinic, Mrs Becker?'

The German woman was polite, but a touch distant. 'No, not today.'

'Fintan's in for a scan.'

Maureen stiffened. She had worked in hospitals long enough to know when someone was a regular face there. *Are you at clinic?* Was she a doctor?

The lift arrived, doors opening. Maureen made a move to file into the rear of the lift where she could stand well back and listen some more. *Beep … Beep* Maureen glanced down — the mobile in her bag was ringing. *Beep … Beep*. She thought she had turned it off. *Beep … Beep*.

Agitated, Maureen yanked out the mobile and answered it. 'Hello …'

'*Mum, for Christ's sake, where have you been?*' It was Brian. '*I've been trying to get hold of you —*'

'Brian …' Maureen could see the lift doors closing. 'Brian, listen, I can't talk to you now …' Her eyes were watching the lights on the lift. 'I'll speak to you later.'

The lights had stopped at the first floor … the second floor … Maureen knew she was losing the German woman.

'*Mum … Mum, what's going on over there?*'

'Later, Brian.' Even as she spoke Maureen was

heading towards the stairs. 'I'll talk to you later, I promise.' She cut the connection and hurried up the stairs.

Brian slammed down the receiver in frustration and turned helplessly to Eva.

'She cut me off.'

Eva was smiling at the shocked expression on his face. 'Oh, come on. It's not that bad.'

'Eva, you don't understand. She's completely lost it. Hasn't got a clue where her mind is. She buggered off to Ireland with Maeve to try and talk to the creditors, but the accountant told me that Dad didn't have any business connections in Ireland.'

'So?'

'So there are no creditors in Ireland for her to talk to.'

Eva looked puzzled. 'Brian, what exactly are you saying?'

Brian threw up his hands in frustration. 'I'm saying that she's completely lost the plot. Doesn't know what the hell she's doing.'

Eva touched his arm. 'Brian, your mother is hurting. She is hurting very badly. Anyone can see that. Perhaps she had some other reason for going to Ireland. Why don't you just leave her be, and give her a break.'

'I'm only trying to help.'

'I know that. But please try and remember that

*you* are not the only one who is hurting and confused right now, she is too.'

'Okay, okay,' Brian exclaimed. 'I hear what you're saying. But, Jesus, Eva, she hasn't got time to waste over in Ireland. In sixty days from now we could lose our home.'

Eva gently touched his arm. 'Do you honestly believe that your mother doesn't also know that?'

'No, I don't believe she does,' Brian said gravely. 'Since Dad's death she doesn't seem to have a clue what she's doing. I've told you, Eva — she's completely lost it!'


Maureen's face was full of panic as she burst breathlessly through the stairwell doors on the second floor of the hospital and started down the corridor, scanning any open rooms, just as she done on the floor below … nowhere.

She could find the German woman nowhere.

Then she saw a notice leading to the private wing … Yes, her ladyship was probably a doctor in the *private* wing. She rushed towards it, pushing open the door and rushing down the corridor, popping her head round every open door …

'Excuse me!'

Maureen turned. A nurse was walking towards her with an expression of suspicious uneasiness on her face.

Maureen's panic was total. 'Sorry, sorry,' she breathed, 'must have the wrong floor.'

She turned and fled down the corridor and out the door like a criminal caught in the act — hearing only the sound of her own breathing and the clatter of her shoes echoing on the stairs as she descended faster and faster ... her mind a mass of confusion, wildly wondering what she would have said to the German woman if she *had* found her inside one of the rooms ...?

# NINE

Bridget Mullen had prepared a lovely evening meal. All the family were gathered around the table in lively chatter. Only Maureen was quiet. She seemed to be listening to everything being said, but her mind was miles away.

'*Mrs Becker*' … that's what the woman waiting for the hospital lift had called her, *Mrs* Becker … So she must be married then. Maybe she was married to the teacher … and then again, maybe she wasn't … Maybe she was just calling herself 'Mrs' because she had a child …

'Uumm! — this is just fabulous, Auntie Bridget.' Maeve was tucking hungrily into the food. 'What's the sauce?'

Bridget looked pleased. 'Onion and leek. Very simple to make. You just heat a knob of butter in the pan and —'

'And open the packet,' said Sean.

Bridget gave him a playful slap across his arm. 'You're not too big to have your arse smacked you know. Maureen — you're not eating.'

Maureen realised she was being spoken to, and smiled. 'Just taking a breather, Bridget.'

Nora raised her wine glass. 'Well, I'd like to

propose a toast. To Maureen and Maeve … Don't be strangers. Come again soon and come often.'

Everyone toasted. Sean leaned across and topped up Maureen's glass. 'So how was Bray?'

'Sorry …' Maureen was completely taken aback.

'Didn't I see you out in Bray this morning?'

'Me? No …' She attempted to laugh it off. 'God, I haven't been to Bray since …' she looked at Nora, 'well, since we were kids.'

Nora grinned, 'Ah, those were the days. Out in Bray running along the edge of the sea. None of us could swim.' She looked at Jenny and Niamh. 'There was no swimming lessons in schools in those days. You lot don't know how lucky you are.'

'So, out in Bray today,' Sean continued, 'I was just sitting there in my cab, about to move off, when I seen —'

'How's your Irish coming along?' Maureen quickly asked Niamh.

'Grand.' Niamh smiled. '*Tabhair dom arán, má sé do thoil é.*'

'What does that mean?'

'Give me a piece of bread, please.'

Bridget lifted the plate of bread and passed it to Niamh. 'Isn't that great, isn't she grand? With Irish like that she could end up becoming the first woman President of Ireland.'

Jenny spluttered with incredulity. 'Granny! We've had two female presidents already. First Mary Robinson, and now Mary McAleese.'

94

'Oh yeah, I forgot about those two.' Bridget made a face. 'It's the Americans that done it. Made me say that. I'm forever reading in the newspapers how the Americans would love to have their first woman president.' She brightened. 'So we're ahead of them there, aren't we? We've led the way there! And if you ask me — that Mary Robinson would make a great president of any country. Where is she now?'

'One of the high-ups in Europe,' Nora replied.

'So you weren't out in Bray today then?' Sean said to Maureen. 'Nowhere near the Dart station?'

Maureen's face flushed — her fair skin coloured easily. She shook her head.

Sean shrugged. 'I could have sworn it was you.'

'No ... no, not me.'

Maeve's eyes were carefully watching her mother's face, certain she was lying.

As soon as dinner was over Maeve slipped upstairs to the bedroom, went straight to the wardrobe and lifted out her mother's hold-all, removing the packet of photographs.

She earnestly studied each picture, sure she had noticed something in one of them that morning. She stopped at a photograph of the woman and boy entering the school ... yes, there it was ... she peered more closely at the words on the elevated board next to the school gate, *St Mary's Primary School, Bray*.

'What are you doing?'

Maeve jerked round — her mother stood stone-faced in the doorway, staring at the photographs and her open hold-all on the bed.

'Looking at these photos,' Maeve replied cheekily. 'I thought you said you hadn't been to Bray?'

Maureen strode forward and snatched up the photographs, her face fuming as she walked over to her own bed and shoved them into her handbag. 'In future you do not poke about in my personal possessions.'

Maeve was unprepared for the strength of her mother's anger. 'I wasn't poking about, I was looking for —'

'If you want money you ask! You don't just take!'

'I wasn't —'

'Don't lie to me!'

'I'm *not* lying.' Tears sprung into Maeve's eyes, her expression shocked and hurt. 'I told you last night, I've got my periods … and this morning I was looking for some tampons …' Maureen suddenly realised the girl was telling the truth.

She couldn't speak, turning away in despair. Is this how bad things had got — taking out her anger on her own children?

She snatched up her handbag, lifted her coat from the chair, and walked to the door.

'Where are you going?' Maeve asked.

'Out,' she replied wearily. 'Out for a walk.'

It was almost dark, a cool wind was blowing gently.

Maureen walked slow and aimlessly, thinking of the long-upheld tradition that had seemed to function quite well in a long-ago society where marriage was marriage and vows were kept, loyalty lasted; and no, it was *not* all right for a man to betray his wife with another woman. Of course many men did, but generally the system had worked, and fewer women got hurt. Fewer children too.

These days, though, anything and everything was allowed, and you'd be shouted out of the room if you dared to criticise the new ways of modern enlightenment. Get yourself strung up for being old-fashioned. A serious danger to the new freedom where, above all, submission was more acceptable than restraint.

No wonder the young girls today suffered all kinds of emotional illnesses, anorexia, bulimia, obesity, depression, mind-anaesthetising drugs …

She looked back to the early years of her marriage when she had — on two or three occasions — been offered the chance of having an affair, and again not so long ago either, just three years ago … a medic at the hospital … but she had resisted, flattered as she had been.

No, she had never thought marriage to be some ludicrous and out-of-date discipline, but a conduct of living, a mutual bonding, a matter of trust, all grounded in the genuine love of one person for another.

But if, in middle-age, one of the partners decided they wanted to move on with someone younger, they should at least have the honesty and integrity to come out in the open and say so, instead of sneaking and cheating and betraying ...

The leaden weight of pain in her breast hurt so much she wanted to sit down somewhere and cry.


It had not been her conscious intention to go to the church, and anyway it was closed. All the childhood days of religiously attending Mass came back to her. *Dominus vobiscum. Et cum spirit to tuo* ... Of course now it was all in English. The Latin was long gone. Along with her faith.

She walked round the side and down the bush-lined path and knocked on the Presbytery door.

Father Cornelius himself opened it. He had become old and grey since Maureen had last seen him. At first he did not recognise her, not until she told him her maiden name.

'Oh, bless my soul! Maureen McDonagh. My God, you've changed!'

'So have you, Father.' Maureen smiled weakly. 'I suppose we both just got older.'

'Ah no, no, I didn't mean it in that way. I meant ... well, you were always such a skinny little thing, but look at you now — still got that same lovely face, but now you have plenty of nice flesh on you, and that blonde hair — why, you look like an older version of Marilyn Monroe!'

'Go on with you!' Maureen grinned. 'But if we're talking about film stars, I suppose you now look like an older version of Spencer Tracy.'

'Ah, that's a pity.' The priest looked genuinely disappointed. 'I always hoped I looked a bit like Paul Newman. But then, vanity, vanity, all is vanity, as the wise Solomon once said. How can I help you, Maureen?'

Maureen hesitated. 'I haven't been to church in years, Father,' she said quietly. 'But, well … I have a problem, and I need someone to talk to.'

Father Cornelius nodded. 'Then you'd better come inside.'

They sat in two armchairs by an unlit fire and talked the whole thing through. Father Cornelius was, as he had always been, sympathetic.

At times Maureen broke down and cried out her anger, at other times she sat rigid, quietly confessing her confusion and her hatred.

Father Cornelius sighed, his words filled with intellectual sorrow. 'Your confusion is understandable, but hatred never helps anyone. Least of all the person doing the hating. Remember what Shakespeare said, 'Heat not a furnace for your foe so hot, that it do burn yourself.'

'Easy for him to say.' Maureen wiped her wet face with the palm of her hand, and gave a small laugh. 'I was expecting you to quote the Bible to me, not Shakespeare.'

'You weren't expecting anything at all, Maureen. You came here in thoughtless desperation, because you had nowhere else to go.'

'Yes, that's true …' Maureen answered honestly. 'I don't really know what I'm doing. Today I followed that woman around like someone half-mad. I still don't know what I hoped to achieve.'

Her hand moved over her breast, unconsciously moving in a pressing motion, as if trying to stop some deep pain.

She said, 'Ever since … ever since I found out, I've had pains all over my body. In my chest, my legs, arms, everywhere.' She smiled wanly. 'The last time I had pains like this, my mother used to say they were growing pains.'

'Growing pains don't end with youth,' Father Cornelius said softly. 'And they are not related only to the body, but the mind and spirit also. They too must be allowed to grow, Maureen, resulting in a broader vision of life, and a stronger acceptance of ourselves. A greater calming. The path of personal inner growth never ends. If it did, life would become stagnant, and so would we. Life, you see, is a never-ending adventure of growing and learning. It has to be. And yes, sometimes it has its pains, but also its rewards.'

'Still,' she said wistfully, 'I wish I was younger.'

'Why?'

'I wish I knew then, what I know now.' She stared towards the window, a wry look on her face.

'You know what rankles the most? Looking back at myself, these past six or seven years, living the life of a fairly contented wife and mother, dealing with all the ups-and-downs of the children, doing the shopping and cleaning before I went to work, or after I finished work, worrying about his clothes, making sure he always had a good appearance in business, carefully ironing his shirts … And all the time he was … Jesus, God!' Tears were spurting down her face. 'Why the hell did I waste twenty-two years of my life on a man like that!'

She stood up. 'I'd better go. It's a long walk back.'

'Will I drive you, Maureen?'

'No, God no, Father Cornelius. I've taken up too much of your time as it is. No, the walk will do me good, maybe even help me to sleep better.'

'Maureen,' he said softly. 'I am a priest, after all. And tonight you have shared your life with me. Your misery. So will you let me say a prayer for you now?'

She wanted to say no, but could not bring herself to refuse, nodding her head in agreement.

Agitated, her face drawn with uneasiness, she stood with him amidst the growing darkness of the room, slowly finding herself being moved by the personal fervour of his quiet prayer for her, a simple and humble supplication to Heaven for her welfare.

His old shoulders were stooped, his black jacket smelled of incense. Her eyes filled with tears when he quietly begged God to give her patience and understanding and, ultimately, a soothing healing, tenderly commending her to the care of Heaven.

When he had concluded, he smiled at her with a kind of sedate regret. 'It's not a prayer that will be answered quickly. Understanding demands answers to questions. And healing takes time.'

She nodded. 'A long time, in my case.'

At the door of the Presbytery, she felt a strange and sudden reluctance to leave. It was fully dark now outside, the wind even cooler, and her pain still consumed her.

She looked at Father Cornelius. 'It's not just the pain of his betrayal I find hard,' she said, 'it's the blatant insult.'


She didn't walk back to the Mullens. She walked to a bridge over the River Liffey and stood staring down at the dark water.

A moment later something hit the water with a gentle splash ... a photograph of the German woman and her son. Another photograph followed it ... and another ... She watched them as they refused to sink, slowly drifting away on the moving surface of the water.

Again the small voice echoed in her mind, *'Daddy's away working ...'*

Tugging the wedding ring from her finger,

Maureen paused for just a moment to stare at the gold band, remembering the day it had been placed on her finger in church, and the sacred vows of love and honour and faithfulness that had accompanied it ... James vowing to 'forsake all others ...'

*'Daddy's away working ... Daddy's away working ....'*

She threw the ring into the Liffey; it sunk instantly. She turned and walked away.

Before she went to sleep that night, something Father Cornelius had said earlier on in their conversation, came back into Maureen's mind.

*'Has it never occurred to you, Maureen, that this woman also may be an innocent victim of your husband's deceit? Maybe she did not know that he was married and had a family in Germany. Maybe he told her the same lies he told you — that he was working in Germany. Just as he told you he was working in Holland. Maybe she is completely unaware of your existence.'*

Maureen did not believe that ... But as the priest had said, maybe, maybe ...

*'Maybe you are being very unfair to her, Maureen.'*

Maybe, maybe ... Maureen shifted uncomfortably in the bed. Easy for him to say. But then ... what if he was right?

A few minutes later a sudden realisation crossed her mind. Tomorrow is a Saturday, she thought. A no-school day.

# TEN

A decision arrived at and acted upon, Maureen stood by the front gate of the bungalow in Bray, listening to the sound of childish laughter. She silently opened the gate and walked into the garden.

'Hello, Jamie.'

Jamie, pedaling his bike on the front lawn, looked round at her, a little wary. She stood looking at his young face. He had a small-boy prettiness to his features, but one day he would be tall and handsome.

'Mam says I mustn't talk to strangers.'

'Well, she's right.' Maureen gave him a reassuring smile. 'I like the bike.'

'Trike. It's a trike. It's got three wheels, see …? My Dad's getting me some stabilizers.'

Maureen's face stiffened. They obviously didn't know James was dead. But they had to find out sometime — as she too had had to find out.

She took a photograph from her purse. 'Is this your Dad, Jamie?'

Jamie got off the trike and took the photograph in his hands, his face lighting up as he laughed. 'Daddy! That's Daddy …'

'Jamie!'

His mother stood in the doorway. She walked forward, speaking to him sharply. 'Come here, Jamie. Now!'

Jamie ran to his mother who steered him protectively behind her back. She looked at Maureen, her expression cold.

'Can I help you?'

'You're German,' Maureen began, 'I can tell by —'

'No, I am *not* German, I am Austrian. Can I help you?'

'Do you know a James Lessing?'

The woman slowly looked Maureen up and down, her eloquent eyebrows arching as she said, 'I'm sorry, but should I know you?'

'Yes. I'm his wife.'

Maureen waited for some reaction, but there was none. The woman didn't even looked embarrassed. She just stood there as if waiting for some further explanation for this visit.

*So the priest had been wrong. This was no innocent victim. She knew everything there was to know, and she didn't give a damn.*

'Did you want something?' she asked.

Maureen couldn't believe her gall. No apology. Nothing.

'Yes,' Maureen said, 'I do want something. An apology would be nice. Something I could tell my children.'

The woman quickly looked at her son. 'Jamie, go

inside please. Now.' She took the photograph from Jamie's hand, looked at it, and ushered him inside. 'Now, Jamie, inside.'

Once the boy had gone inside, she turned back to Maureen. 'I'm sorry, but any problem you have with James has got nothing to do with myself or my son.'

She walked over to Maureen, offering her the photograph back. Maureen ignored it.

'But Jamie is his son, isn't he?'

'That's none of your business.'

'Oh, I think it is. You see, James Lessing was my husband for twenty-two years. I thought he was a faithful husband. And my children believe he was their devoted father, and theirs only.'

'I told you, whatever your problem, you must speak to James, not me.'

'I can't speak to James,' Maureen said bluntly. 'He's dead.'

The woman finally showed some emotion. 'Dead? No …' She shook her head suspiciously. 'You're lying.'

'No.' Maureen's face was implacable. 'That's the brutal truth I've just told you. I am his wife, and he is dead.'

Maureen knew she could have been gentler, but she wanted to hurt this woman, hurt her *hard*.

The woman's aloof posture slumped before Maureen's eyes. 'Oh, God … Dead? … How?'

'A heart attack. After he got off the flight back

from Holland — or as I now know — the flight back from Dublin.'

'Has he …'

'Yes. His children cried terribly at his funeral. They thought it was the pressure of his work that killed him.'

'Oh God …' the woman gave a low moan of pain and stumbled backwards, reaching blindly for the fence to steady herself. 'Oh, God …'

'Could you tell me your name,' Maureen said matter-of-factly.

'Liza … Liza Becker … Did James not —'

'No, he didn't tell me your name. He didn't tell me anything about you. And you *know* he didn't.'

'Mam! Mam …' Jamie came out of the house, his face full of confusion as he rushed to comfort his mother. 'Don't cry, Mam …'

'Wait!' Liza shouted. 'Don't go! I want to know —' But Maureen was walking away, ignoring the anguished cries behind her.


Two hours later, back at the Mullens, Maeve stood watching her mother roughly shoving piles of clothes into an open suitcase.

'I don't understand. Why all the sudden rush?'

'Just do as I ask, please. Get your things out of the wardrobe and start packing. We're leaving on the next flight.'

'But *why?*'

'Because I've done what I had to do here,' Maureen said grimly. 'And now I'm finished with Ireland. Now it's time for me to go back to Germany and try and save our home.'

'But, Mum —'

'Look, Maeve, why don't you go downstairs and get yourself a sandwich and a cup of tea before we leave,' Maureen said wearily. 'I'll finish the packing. No, no arguments now. Go on, go on …'

She dismissed Maeve with a turn of her back, lifting out clothes from the wardrobe and throwing them into the suitcase without even folding them.


Rain was battering against the conservatory windows. Maeve walked in to find Nora holding a step-ladder for Sean who was struggling to fix a small leak in the conservatory roof.

'Jayz, will you listen to that?' Sean shouted down. 'It's a bloody monsoon.'

'And most of it's on my floor,' Bridget replied wryly. 'And where did it come from? There was no rain this morning.'

Turning round, Bridget saw Maeve and snapped into action. 'I'll make you something to eat, love. Is your mother coming down? Or shall I send something up?'

'I don't think she wants anything,' Maeve said, an excusing plea on her face. 'She's a bit pushed, you know … wanting to catch the next flight.'

'She's got to eat.' Bridget frowned. 'Sure she hasn't eaten more than a pick since she came here.'

'Bridget, she's fine,' Nora said firmly. 'She doesn't have to eat if she doesn't want to.' Nora quickly changed the subject, smiling at Maeve. 'So, I hear you met some admirers the other day? Followed around by three lads.'

'Me?' Maeve went red with embarrassment. 'Those three lads? It was Jenny. She kept smiling at them.'

'Now I wonder where Jenny got that from?' said Sean Mullen, looking down at Maeve with a twinkle in his eyes. 'Her mother was just the same, you know. Always smiling at me and gasping for a piece of my body.'

Nora laughed. 'I was not!'

'Just as well it wasn't your brain she was after,' Bridget commented. 'She'd have been sadly disappointed.'

Sean looked over at his mother. 'Why would she?'

'Because you've got no brain. They told me that when you were born. "Mrs Mullen," says they, "he's got everything except a brain. We hope you don't mind."'

'Ha, ha. Very funny you ain't, Mother.'

The front doorbell buzzed loudly. 'I'll get that.' Bridget threw down her tea-towel. 'It's probably the Belgians.'

The buzzing continued relentlessly. 'Yes, alright,

hold your horses, I'm coming,' Bridget shouted. 'No need to get in such a panic!'

She hauled open the door. A man in his thirties stood drenched on the doorstep. Bridget eyed his dripping hair and sodden jacket.

'I'm sorry, we're fully booked.'

'I'm looking for a woman. Maureen Lessing ...?'

He was pacing up and down the floor of the Guest Lounge when Maureen reached the door and saw who it was. The teacher from the school. She was about to turn away, but then he saw her.

'Maureen Lessing?'

'That's me,' she replied, her voice brittle.

'Mrs Lessing, I need to talk to you about Liza Becker. I'd like you to tell me what's going on?'

Maureen was surprised by his directness. 'Why don't you ask her?'

'I can't. The doctor has her under sedation.'

Maureen frowned. Surely he wasn't expecting her to feel any kind of sympathy for that woman.

'So?'

'She's got a five-year-old child, for God's sake. The boy's hysterical. Now, please, Mrs Lessing, will you tell me what's going on here?'

Maureen regarded him coldly. 'You're a stranger to me. I don't have to discuss anything with you.'

He seemed to realise that. 'Yes, I know, I'm sorry

110

… my name is Michael Docherty. Liza is a friend of mine. Her son is at my school.'

'So?' Maureen repeated.

'Look, I'm only trying to help.'

*Oh, that old phrase again.*

'And just who are you trying to *help?*' she snapped. 'Not me, that's for sure. I've got two children, Mr Docherty. Will you help me to tell them? Will you *help* me to explain to them about their father having another family here in Ireland? Another family he's had for years!'

Michael Docherty stared at her, completely thrown. 'You mean … you didn't know?'

'Know? Of course I didn't know! What do you think I'm doing here?'

'I don't understand.' Michael Docherty looked acutely embarrassed. 'Liza said you and James were separated.'

Maureen smiled sneeringly. 'So that's the story she's been spinning you, is it?'

The teacher didn't seem to know what to think. 'Are you saying that Liza's been lying about all this?'

'Work it out for yourself, man,' Maureen snapped. 'He came to Ireland no more than once a month. He spent most of his life in Germany. A separated man would have had more time to spare. All his phone calls to her were from his mobile, never his home. And she, too, must have always called him on his mobile, never at his home number.

111

It was all done *sneakily*, all done in secret, d'you hear?'

'But —' he tried to protest.

'So yes, I *am* saying she's been lying to you,' Maureen continued furiously. 'And by the looks of it, she took you in hook, line and sinker. So don't you *dare* come here and tell me that you're only trying to *help*. You can't help me or my children! You have no idea the financial mess James left us in because of the huge sums of money he kept giving to that woman — huge cash withdrawals every month. And I'm not prepared now to waste any more of my time with another of Liza Becker's lackeying men.'

She turned away dismissively and walked towards the stairs. Michael Docherty followed her. 'Mrs Lessing, please … Look, something is very wrong here.'

'What is wrong, Mr Docherty, is that for twenty-two years I was married to a man who betrayed me and his two children — and now you want me to feel sorry for the woman who helped him to do it.'

'Liza didn't help him to betray you, Mrs Lessing. She thought you were separated. She did! I'm sure of it. That's what your husband told her. He said you wouldn't give him a divorce. He said you didn't love him, but you wouldn't let him go. That's what he told her. So if he betrayed you, then he betrayed her also.'

*God, you're pathetic*, Maureen thought. *One of her pathetic drooling fools, just like James was.*

112

'Mum?'

Maureen froze when Maeve appeared. Her daughter's eyes were shooting quizzical looks at Michael Docherty. 'Oh. Sorry …'

'Did you want something, Maeve?'

'Yeah … Sean's getting a bit concerned about the time.'

'I'm just coming.'

'Right.'

There was an awkward silence as they waited for Maeve to go, and in that silence a thought struck Maureen.

'How did you know where I was staying?' she asked curiously. 'I didn't give my address to that woman, so how did you find me? And so quickly?'

'Well, I knew your name. And Liza has said in the past that you lived near Düsseldorf. So I got onto Directory Enquiries. They gave me your number there. I spoke to your son. But it's alright, I didn't tell him any—'

'You did *what?*' Maureen was stunned by the audacity of it. This fellow was as bad and mischievous as that Becker bitch. 'You rang my home and spoke to my son? You've no right! How dare —'

'Mrs Lessing, please. I'm just trying to help.'

'Then help yourself to go home, Mr Docherty! And from now on, leave me and my family alone.'

She turned and walked up the stairs. Michael

Docherty stared after her helplessly, realising he had overstepped his mark, and only succeeded in making matters a great deal worse.

Maeve had gone up to the bedroom. She stood by the window watching Michael Docherty as he walked down the street to his car.

A moment later Maureen entered the room, unable to look Maeve in the face. She crossed quickly to the bed and picked up the suitcase with trembling hands. 'We'll be late if we don't rush.'

'It's Dad, isn't it?' Maeve said quietly. 'That man, he told you something about Dad, didn't he?'

Maureen lowered the suitcase, and sat down on the bed wearily. 'No, he came about something to do with the business.'

'You don't have to pretend anymore,' Maeve said. 'It's all right, Mum, I'm not a child. I know everything about Dad's other woman.'

Stunned, Maureen stared at her daughter. 'How long have you known?'

'Oh, ages.' Maeve pretended matter-of-factness and shrugged. 'Half the kids in my class, their parents are either divorced or splitting up. And then I found those photos … Dad was having an affair, wasn't he?'

When Maureen made no answer, Maeve persisted, 'He was, wasn't he?'

Maureen was sitting with a sorely puzzled

expression on her face. 'But I thought you said you knew all about it?'

'I lied,' Maeve admitted quietly, her speech beginning to tremble. 'So, is it true?'

Maureen nodded, standing up and taking Maeve's hands in both of her own, struggling to contain her own emotions and find the right words to explain.

'Your dad … He met someone else … They have a child. A boy of five.'

Maeve snatched her hand away, confused and angry. She obviously had never really believed it could be true.

'Why didn't you tell *us* about it? Me and Brian? We were entitled to know.'

'I didn't know about it myself,' Maureen said. 'I only found out after he died.'

'So if it weren't for his heart attack, he'd probably still be flitting back and forth between us and them?'

'Yes, I suppose so. It's what's he did for at least five years.'

'And this other woman — what's she like?'

Maureen shrugged. 'All I know is what I've managed to find out. Her name is Becker. Liza Becker. She lives in Bray. She's foreign, Austrian.'

'How did he meet her?'

'Maeve, I really don't know any more than I've just told you.'

Downstairs in the kitchen, Sean Mullen was jangling his keys. 'I'm telling you, they're going to miss the bloody plane.'

'Will you stop doing that?' Bridget snapped.

'Doing what?'

'Jangling your keys like a restless jailer.'

'I know it doesn't mean a sweet damn to anyone here except myself,' Sean said with an aggrieved air, 'but I'm booked for another fare in two hours.'

Bridget suddenly said, 'Nora, I don't suppose with you being Maureen's best friend and all, you would happen to know what Maureen's playing at?'

Nora looked up from the newspaper she had been pretending to read to cover her anxiety. 'What do you mean — playing at?'

'Well, for instance, that Mickey-Dazzler who came calling at the door looking for her. He seemed —'

'I know nothing about him,' Nora cut her short. 'He was probably some old business acquaintance of Maureen's husband, come to pay his respects to his widow.'

Sean gave an insightful look to his mother. 'Still strictly taboo, so it is, Mother,' he said dryly. 'Any questions to Nora about Maureen are still strictly taboo.'

Maeve was getting very upset, tears streaming down her face.

'What I don't understand is … if Dad didn't love you, if he didn't love us, why didn't he just leave? I mean, he *could* have just left, couldn't he?'

'Yes, he could have left us at any time. I would not have stopped him. And he knew that.'

'So *why*? I mean, for God's sake, we thought he was just our dad! That's why we laughed off all the things about him that aggravated us. Because he was our dad. But we didn't know he was someone else's dad too! Brian'll freak out! Do people in Bray think that woman is Dad's *wife*?'

'I don't know.'

Maeve was sobbing brokenly now. 'Dad could have at least told me I had another brother … I want to meet him. I want to go to Bray and meet him. I want to understand —'

'*No!*' Maureen cried, angrily grabbing Maeve by the shoulders. 'Maeve, listen to me, I don't want you to go anywhere near Bray! That woman and her son are *nothing* to us! Do you understand that — *nothing*!'

Maeve was cringing back against her mother's rage, tears spilling down her face. 'Oh, love …' Maureen tried to hug her daughter, but Maeve broke away from her and ran furiously out of the bedroom.

'*Maeve … Maeve …!*'

Sean Mullen heard Maureen's distant shouts a few seconds before he heard the slamming of the front door.

117

'What in God's name is going on now?'

Nora sprang to her feet. 'It's all right, Sean. Leave it to me.'

'Listen,' said Sean, irritated, 'all joking aside now — I want to know what's going on?'

'Nothing,' Nora replied over her shoulder. 'Everything's fine.' And then she was gone.

Sean gestured to his mother in hopeless resignation and tossed his car keys onto the table. 'Everything's fine, she says. So why am I hanging around here? Because no way are they going to make that plane now.'

'Not now,' Bridget agreed.

'And who was that fella who came here looking for Maureen? Did he say anything to you about why he wanted to see her?'

'No.' Bridget narrowed her eyes and said conspiratorially, 'But d'you know what I think? I think Maureen has got herself a new man friend, so I do.'

'A what? Sure she's only widowed a few weeks, for God's sake.' Sean stared at Bridget as if she was mad. 'Have you been drinking that funny herbal tea again?'

Nora opened the front door to see a distressed Maureen standing in the rain in the empty street.

'Maureen … For God's sake. What's wrong?'

'Nothing, nothing,' Maureen answered, distraught. 'It's just Maeve and me … we had a row.'

'A row bad enough to make her go running out in the pouring rain?'

Nora put an arm around Maureen's shoulders, real concern in her eyes. 'Listen, there's more to all this than you've told me. You've been acting very odd these past few days. And young Maeve's been upset about something since yesterday morning. So what's going on?'

Maureen's shame was almost childlike. 'If I tell you the truth, Nora ... you won't tell anyone, will you?'

Nora could see the truth was serious, something bad and shameful. What had Maureen done? She nodded towards her Puegot parked a few feet away. 'Let's get in the car and talk in the dry.'

'Is it open?'

Nora lifted the long chain of keys hanging down from her neck. 'It will be in a sec. Come on.'

Inside the car, Maureen began to tell her friend everything. Nora was visibly shocked. 'Jesus Christ ...'

Then later, as the full story unfolded, Nora's main emotion was anger. 'I have to say it, Maureen, but that husband of yours was a ripe bastard, wasn't he?'


*Run, run, run!* Through the pouring rain Maeve was fleeing blindly. All she wanted to do was run far away from her mother whom she now hated beyond all reason. She didn't know exactly *why* she hated her, she just did.

But she knew where she was going — to Bray. She sprinted down the steps of the Dart station and wondered what she would do when she got there.

From the back pocket of her jeans she pulled out the neatly folded five-pound-note her mother had given to her in case of an emergency, and paid for her ticket.

On the train she stared through the rain-misted window remembering something she had overheard the man saying to her mother. *I knew your name ... so I got onto Directory Enquiries ....*

At Bray, Maeve came out of the station and stood looking helplessly around her to get her bearings.

She started walking towards the seafront, oblivious of the rain, her eyes searching until she found a telephone kiosk outside an amusement arcade.

She pulled open the door and stepped in out the rain and began searching through the telephone directory.

'Becker. Liza Becker ... It wasn't exactly a common Irish name ...

Sean Mullen just gaped when Nora popped her head round the kitchen door and announced that Maeve had gone missing.

'Gone where?' Sean grabbed his keys from the table. 'Jesus, Nora, if I have to wait here for much longer I'll be shaking hands at my own funeral. So come on, let's go find her!'

Nora flashed up her hand. 'No, no, it's all right, Sean. Maureen thinks she knows where Maeve might have gone. It'll be quicker if I drive her. Won't be long.'

Sean stared after her, then turned his head and stared at his mother. 'Can you beat that?'

Bridget smiled conspiratorially. 'Maeve and Maureen only had their row after that man came here. That's why Maeve's upset. She doesn't like the idea of a new man taking the place of her daddy in her mother's affections. And so soon after her daddy's death too.'

Sean considered this for a long moment, then said solemnly, 'In all our discussions about family life, it was my father's general opinion that you had a slate loose in your roof, Mother. Or as he used to put it "too many bats in your thatch.'

Bridget smiled, undeterred. 'Your father used to say that *all* women had a slate loose. He was a male chauvinist, of course, like yourself.'


Nora was driving along Bray's rainswept seafront road. 'Listen, Maureen, maybe you should talk to this woman. It could be that this Michael character is telling the truth.'

'I've already spoken to her,' Maureen replied coldly. 'And I know the truth.'

'God, this rain is awful ...' Nora had the windshield wipers going at full speed. 'Are you sure this is where Maeve came?'

Maureen shook her head, helpless to think otherwise. 'Where else would she go?'


Maeve had reached the bungalow where Liza Becker lived, standing outside the front door.

She took a deep breath and knocked.

No reply.

She knocked again.

Not a sound of anyone coming to the door.

Where were they? Maybe that man had come back and driven them off somewhere, back to his own house even?

Confused, Maeve walked to one of the windows and peered through the glass. It looked like somebody's study or workroom ... She could see a computer, an expensive one, the type her father used. And standing next to it, a large framed photograph of her father with his other family ... a big smile on his face ... all three of them smiling happily for the camera.

Maeve's feeling of revulsion against her father was so strong she was almost sick. *Look at him — as if me and Brian and Mum didn't exist!*

The tears in her eyes obscured her mother's

reflection in the window as Maureen walked up behind her.

'Maeve …'

Maeve turned round slowly, her clothes completely drenched through, her long hair stringy and dripping wet around her face.

'Maeve …' Maureen almost sobbed as she reached out to her daughter.

Maeve moved meekly into her mother's arms, tears mingling with the rain on her young face. 'I want to go home now,' she said. 'Home to Germany.'


In the kitchen, Nora nodded to Sean. 'They'll be ready to go in five minutes. They've just got to change into something dry.'

'As a matter of historical fact,' Sean said, poker-faced, 'aeroplanes usually leave at the time they are scheduled to leave. They do not hang around waiting for any late passengers. That's not their code.'

Nora glanced at her watch. 'But it's only ten minutes to four. The plan's not scheduled to leave until five-thirty.'

'I thought you said it was leaving at four-thirty?'

'No, that's the check-in time. If we leave now we can still get there about half-an-hour before departure, earlier maybe, if you put your foot down.'

Sean sighed, and lifted his keys from the table. 'D'you know something —'

'Yes, I do,' Nora interrupted, walking over to Sean and giving him a kiss, a strange expression on her face. 'As husbands go, I know I've got myself one of the best.'

# ELEVEN

The roar of the Aer Lingus jet as it descended towards the runway at Düsseldorf Express Airport made Maureen think of James's last flight, leaving his secret family in Dublin to return to his conventional family in Germany. What had he been thinking on that flight? And what *would* he have been thinking — if he had known what lay waiting for him on the autobahn?

The wheels of the aircraft touched the ground in a series of bumps which seemed to jolt Maeve out of her quietness.

'Brian will freak about all this,' she said.

'Don't worry,' Maureen murmured. 'I'll explain it all to him.'

'Yeah, and be dead honest with him, Mum, no hedging. Just tell him the whole truth.'

'I don't know the whole truth. I only know part of it.' Maureen glanced sideways at her daughter. 'And I don't want to know any more. I just want to get on with my life now.'

In the taxi home, Maeve asked, 'Are you going to carry on with your driving lessons?'

Maureen thought about it. 'No, I don't think I'll bother. No point, really. Not without a car.'

Maureen was full of thought as she paid off the taxi and walked up to the front door. Could she really let them take away this house? Or could she fight them?

'I'm not giving it up without a fight,' she said determinedly, more to herself than to Maeve. 'There must be a way round it somehow.'

The front door opened. Eva stood there, caught by surprise. 'Oh, hi ...' She called over her shoulder. 'Brian, your Mum's home!'

'What!' Brian rushed into the hall, staring at his mother. 'Why didn't you call?'

'Why?' Maureen asked wryly. 'Do I *need* to call and ask permission before I return to my own home?'

'No, no ...' Brian was suddenly full of smiles. 'What I meant was, I'd have met you at the airport. Here, that suitcase looks heavy, give it to me.'

Maureen followed him into the hall, glancing quickly over her shoulder to give Maeve an astonished *'He's actually carrying my suitcase for me!'* look.

In the kitchen, Brian astonished her even more by making her a cup of tea.

She stood looking around in amazement at the spotless kitchen. 'Brian, did you do all this?'

'Well, no ... Eva helped.' He handed her the tea. 'You should have told me, you know.'

'Told you what?'

Brian looked at her steadily. 'Why can't you be honest with me?'

Maureen was not ready for this, not yet. A breather. A cup of tea. Time to sit down and prepare her words. She hedged.

'Honest with you about what?'

'Well for a start, Michael Docherty?'

'Michael Docherty?'

'Exactly. Who the hell is he?'

Maureen's face tightened with tension. Had Michael Docherty lied to her and told Brian everything? In fact, just what *had* he told Brian?

'What did Michael Docherty tell you?'

'Nothing. He just gave me a load of old blarney. I thought it might have something to do with Dad's business … But then Dad didn't have any business connections in Ireland, did he?'

She looked at him.

'So why the lie?' Brian asked.

Maureen sat down in growing hopelessness and dejection. He was not giving her any time.

'Brian, believe it or not, everything I have done, all the things I have not told you, it's because I was trying very hard to protect you.'

'From what? And why do I need protecting? I'm not Maeve. I'm nineteen.'

'I know, but some things … well …' Oh why the hell hadn't he given her time to prepare her words.

'Well?' Brian demanded.

'Well,' she said simply. 'You have a brother.'

Later that night she knocked on the door of Brian's room. He had retreated there only minutes after she had told him the whole truth.

He opened the door to her and pretended adjustment, sitting down on the bed, very calm.

'Are you all right?' she asked quietly.

'I'm fine,' Brian replied, shrugging it off, 'because it doesn't really matter now, does it?'

'No.'

'That kid. He may be Dad's spawn, but he's not my brother. Like you said, they're nothing to us. That woman and her son. Nothing.'

'Nothing,' Maureen repeated. 'And from now on we must carry on with our lives as before, as if they didn't exist.'

But they did exist. And in the following few weeks the reality of their existence was not only brought home to every member of the Lessing family, but became a fact that was inescapable.

# TWELVE

The plaque on the wall behind Major Pinkerton's desk read: *Ask the impossible, achieve the maximum.*

Maureen stood smiling at it, glad to be back at work. She lifted the pile of unopened mail from the desk and carried it through to her own office, to find another pile of unopened mail.

She was sorting the mail into some semblance of order when Major Pinkerton appeared in the doorway, beaming at her.

'Mrs Maureen Lessing, as I live and breath! And it looks like you've returned just in time.'

'I can see that.' Maureen smiled, indicating the pile of post. 'You're a soldier, I thought you lot were supposed to be organised.'

The major gave the post a cursory glance. 'Yes, sorry about that. We've had a bit of a flap on. The psychiatric ward. It was closed last week. Orders from on high.'

'What!' Maureen stared at him. 'But I thought it was still under review?'

'So did I.' He shrugged. 'We're clearly surplus to requirements. It looks like the whole place is in line for the chop.'

'What about the Base?'

'They're running it down. The cold war is over and so by the looks of it are we.' He gave her a grim smile. 'Sorry.'

Maureen's shock was plain. She had intended to ask him for a rise in salary but that was now out of the question.

*So what do I say to the bank now?* she wondered.


Maeve was late for school and she didn't care. There was nothing, after all, nothing in her life now that wasn't completely ruined. They had no money, the house would probably have to be sold — and if her friends at school ever found out about her dad!

She shut the front door behind her and double-locked it as usual, pausing for a long moment with her key still in the lock ... feeling a strange sensation on her back ... an odd intuition that someone was watching her.

She turned her head sharply and looked: the street was empty, not a soul in sight.

She walked curiously down the path, wondering why she had conjured up such a notion?

Maybe she was in the early stages of having a nervous breakdown? She could be, nervous breakdowns were very common these days. Other kids in her school were always taking time off to go to counselling sessions because of the trauma of their parents' divorce.

I deserve time off too, Maeve thought self-pityingly. I'm completely traumatised.

She decided to skip school, but didn't know where else to go. The streets were quite empty as she made her way towards the park. The sun was shining directly in front of her, bursting out in all directions, illuminating the greenness of the trees.

She squinted at the sun and felt a slow resentment towards it, wishing it would bugger off behind a cloud. She wanted a dark sky and leafless trees to match the greyness of her mood.

Not that anyone had even *noticed* how completely traumatised she was, she thought sullenly, fumbling in her bag for her secret pack of cigarettes. The only person Mum really cared about was Brian. And the only person Brian really cared about was himself.

She stuck a cigarette in her mouth and impatiently rifled through her bag. Damn! No matches.

Further up the park's path she came to the children's play area and saw two Turkish lads messing about on the swings. With them was a blonde German girl smoking a cigarette.

Maeve sauntered up to the girl. 'Got a light?'

'Sure.' The girl took a lighter from the pocket of her jeans and flicked it against Maeve's cigarette. The cupped flame was like a beacon of friendship. Maeve smiled her thanks, then noticed the girl had three small gold rings pierced into her right eyebrow.

Her admiration was instant. 'Cool.' She nodded towards the rings and asked the girl, 'Where did you get them done?'

The girl told her where.

'Did they use a gun or a needle?' Maeve asked the German girl.

'They only use guns when piercing the ears,' the girl replied. 'Everywhere else it is best to have the needle. More slow, more painful, but it heals much quicker. Cleaner too.'

'Have you been pierced anywhere else?'

The girl smiled and nodded, glancing over at the two Turkish lads. '*Ja,* but I'm not going to tell you where.'

The lads were more interested in Maeve's cigarettes. She gave them one each, then one to the girl, but as soon as they were lit up, the three lost interest in Maeve and decided to move on.

*They think I'm just a kid,* Maeve thought as she watched them drift away. *Or maybe they just think I look middle-class and boring.* The rejection hurt, deepening her sense of inferiority. There had to be something wrong with her, and something wrong with Brian too. Why else had their father secretly rejected them and gone off to start a new family elsewhere. What had she done that had been so wrong? Hadn't she always shown him how much she loved him? Yes, always. And every birthday and Father's Day she had bought him a present and a card for 'The Best Dad in the World'. So *why* had he done it? And *why* had he given all his money to that woman? Not caring if they lost the house. Not caring about her or Brian or Mum at all.

She turned away from the swings and sauntered back down the path, deciding to go home, walking heavily, wishing it would rain, wishing someone would notice how utterly devastated she was.

Overwhelmed with despondency and tear-jerking compassion for herself, she turned into her road, taking out the house-keys and deciding to spend the rest of the morning lying on the sofa watching TV with a bowl of Special K.

Suddenly she caught sight of a man in their garden. He was leaning over the rubbish bin, searching inside, shoving pieces of paper into his pockets.

For a moment Maeve just stared ... he was a fairly well-dressed man, not a tramp searching for food. So what the hell was he doing?

'Hey!' she shouted.

The man looked round, saw her, then turned and walked away very quickly.

Nervously, Maeve continued walking along the pavement until she reached the house — then dashed to the door and rushed inside. There was something about the man that was spooky.

She went straight to the phone to call her mother, then stopped, realising she couldn't do that. No way. Her mother would go bananas if she knew she had skipped off school.

But what was the man *doing?* Stealing bits of dirty paper from the bin? Shoving them into his pocket.

Maybe he's just a crazy, she thought. Maybe he goes round stealing from everyone's rubbish bins.

Slowly she moved back to the front door and put her eye to the spy-hole, but the garden was deserted, and the man was definitely gone.

Just a crazy, she decided.

Maureen returned home that evening laden down with bags of groceries, calling out from the hall, 'Maeve. I'm home.'

Brian's voice answered from the study. 'Maeve's not here.'

Maureen struggled to the door of the study and looked in. Brian glanced up at her, but made no effort to help with her bags.

'Maeve's gone out,' he said coolly. 'Eva's here. Upstairs. Washing her hair. She'll be down in a minute.'

Brian turned back to the documents in front of him on the desk, looking every inch his father, like the man who now owned the house. 'Oh, by the way,' he added, 'I've had the house valued.'

'You've *what*?' Maureen stared at him in disbelief.

'Here,' he said coolly, lifting a letter and handing it to her. She put down the bags, took the letter and read it. The valuation figure shocked her.

'Don't panic,' Brian said. 'The guy who did the valuation is a friend of mine. He did it as a favour. It's just a precaution. You see, the trick is, if we get a low valuation, the bank is much less likely to force us to sell.

'And you went to the bank, didn't you?' Maureen said stonily. 'Hans told me. You went to the bank — behind my back.'

'No! I mean, I did, yes. But I was trying to telephone you in Ireland, wasn't I? I couldn't get through on your mobile.'

Eva appeared beside Maureen in the doorway. 'Anyone want coffee?'

Maureen bit back her anger. These two seemed to have taken over the place while she was away. It felt like another house, like it had nothing to do with her. She was beginning to feel as if she had lost whatever authority she once had.

She looked pointedly at Brian. 'Is there anything else I should know, or is that it?'

Brian sighed patiently. 'Look, Mum, don't worry about the bank. The bank will do a deal. They all do — we just have to make them an offer.'

Maureen could have told him her latest news, that she was facing possible redundancy, but she didn't bother. She picked up her bags and walked past Eva into the kitchen.

As she dumped the bags on the table, Eva followed her in, walking over to the sink and filling the kettle. She switched it on, then turned and reached for one of the shopping bags.

'Do you want me to help you unpack?'

Maureen's smile was tight. 'I do know where everything goes, Eva. Thank you.'

Eva was immediately aware of the tension and eased back, giving Maureen her own space.

Brian barged in. 'Here, come on, we'll *all* do it.'

'I can do it myself, Brian,' Maureen insisted.

'Oh, come on, Mum, you're tired. Give yourself a break.' He began unpacking. 'Right, where does this lot go then?'

Maureen's face was white with anger. He was dominating her as if she was some doddering old fool.

Eva said diplomatically. 'Brian, I think your Mum would prefer to do it herself.'

Brian ignored her. 'Kitchen stuff — under the sink.'

Eva reached out and firmly touched his arm. 'Brian!'

He savagely jerked his arm away, turning on Eva as if she was a traitor. 'Don't you interfere in this, alright? I mean, Jesus, whose side are you on?'

Eva stared at him, astonished. 'I didn't know we were taking sides ... My God, what's wrong with you?' She walked out of the kitchen. Seconds later the front door slammed.

Brian made no attempt to follow her. He turned back to the groceries on the table and continued unpacking.

'She'll come back,' he murmured confidently. 'She always does.'

Maureen stood silent, mystified and dismayed. It seemed coping with Brian was going to be yet another problem she had not foreseen.

At seven o'clock Maeve returned. The smell of home cooking filled the air. It cheered Maeve instantly; she was famished. She had spent the past two hours at her friend Katrin's house, asking her all the details of the trauma of her parents' divorce.

Katrin had insisted it had destroyed her totally, and since then she had been secretly suffering from anorexia.

Maeve had been amazed to hear that, because Katrin was quiet fat and didn't look a bit thinner than she had looked before the divorce. In fact, she looked even fatter, bursting out in all directions — just like the sun earlier.

'Is that you, Maeve?' her mother called from the kitchen.

The kitchen table was already set. A frying pan full of lamb chops was sizzling on the stove. Her mother was bent down, lifting out a tray of roast potatoes from the oven.

'Hi, Mum.'

Her mother glanced round. 'I was beginning to get worried. Where have you been?'

'Round at Katrin's.' Maeve's eyes popped at the

sight of freshly-baked golden scones on the side unit. 'You've baked scones! You haven't done that for ages.'

Her mother smiled gently. 'I remembered how much you liked them, Maeve. So I just got stuck in and baked some for you. How was school?'

'School?' Maeve averted her eyes guiltily. 'Fine ... Oh, yeah, a funny thing, though,' she added, changing the details slightly. 'When I was going out this morning I saw a man searching in our rubbish bin.'

Maureen looked at her dubiously. 'Searching in our rubbish bin? Was he a tramp?'

'No.' Maeve shook her head. 'He was a crazy.'


Maureen arrived into work early the following morning and was soon typing away at her computer, very swiftly, very efficiently, endeavouring to catch up with the back-log caused by her time away in Ireland. A raise may have been out of the question but her job wasn't lost yet. So far it was only the psychiatric ward they were closing down.

Still, it worried her.

The phone on her desk rang. She picked up the receiver, jamming it behind her ear, allowing her to continue typing as she talked.

'Hello, Major Pinkerton's secretary ...'

'Maureen, it's Hans. I've been trying to get hold of you. About the house.'

She stopped typing, her expression stiffening. 'What about the house, Hans? What's wrong?'

'It looks like our friends at the Bank are about to get heavy. So we have to meet, Maureen, and decide what to do.'

In his own office, Major Pinkerton also received a telephone call that alarmed him.

He sat forward in his chair and frowned. 'Who exactly am I speaking to?'

As he listened to the voice at the other end of the line, the major's face began to turn red with indignation.

'No, I most certainly can *not*!' he replied sharply. 'This is a *military* hospital and we never reveal information about our personnel to any outside civilian body!'

Two minutes later he slammed down the phone and went looking for Maureen. He found her down the corridor, struggling to sort out the foibles of the new vending machine.

She turned her head to him and shrugged. 'This thing doesn't work. Shall I go back and put the kettle on and make our coffee as usual?'

'Maureen,' he said in a hushed, conspiratorial tone, 'I've just had a man on the phone asking some very personal questions about you ...'

Maureen met Hans Reiner at six o'clock in a city

lounge bar. It was a dark place, with heavy wood-panelled walls and upholstered red-velvet seating.

Under normal circumstances Maureen would have felt slightly uncomfortable amongst the suited businessmen and their mobile phone conversations, but today she didn't care — too shocked by what Hans was telling her.

'They're called *"umfassende Uberprufung"* ... I don't know the correct English term,' Hans continued, 'but it's like ... well, they do a complete search. Hidden surveillance, everything. Basically, the bank employs someone to check that you are not hiding anything from them.'

Maureen was appalled. 'But can they do that? I mean, it's disgusting! Going through my rubbish, phoning up my work, and God knows what else they've done.'

'You owe them money. A lot of money. Unfortunately it makes them nervous. They think maybe you could have other assets that you have not told them about, and this is how they find out.'

'I have no other assets!' Maureen was exasperated. 'This is all Brian's fault. He should never have gone to the bank. He should never have got a false low valuation. He should have minded his own business and left mine for me to deal with.'

'He just wants to help, Maureen.'

'Help!' Maureen fumed. 'Why does everyone think they have a right to barge into other people's

140

business with the excuse that they are just trying to help?'

She thought of Michael Docherty, another audacious helper. 'Just barge right in demanding answers.' Maureen was feeling wildly angry. 'The trouble is, it's never *me* they really want to help. It's either someone else or themselves.'

She put down her glass and gathered up her things. 'I should go.'

Hans quickly intercepted her. 'Look, why don't you let me buy you supper. Do you like sushi? There is a very good Japanese restaurant around the corner.'

'No, really, thank you, Hans, but I can't. Maeve will be at home waiting for me and her dinner.'

'Some other night, then?' Hans touched her arm, his expression serious. 'But you know, Maureen, if you need anything, or if you feel lonely, need to talk, or even if you would just like a nice meal away from the family … give me a call. I'll always be here for you, Maureen, you know that.'

What she knew was that Hans was hinting at something more than friendship. She could scarcely believe it, but she hid her surprise behind a tentative smile.

'Will you do that, Maureen? Will you call me?'

She nodded. 'As a friend, Hans. Just as a friend, okay?'

'I'll drive you home.'

'No, no, there's no need.'

Hans stood up and took her arm. 'Come on, Maureen, I insist.'

She allowed him to lead her out, her mind wondering why every male in her life insisted on treating her as if she was incapable of doing anything without their help.

The only one who seemed to trust her completely, and respect her intelligence, was her boss, Major Pinkerton.

# THIRTEEN

In Ireland, Liza Becker was also fuming inwardly as she lifted a tray of chicken kiev out of the oven.

The kitchen behind her was spotless and sterile, due to her constant war against every species of germ. The doors and surfaces of every kitchen unit, the white formica table, and every single one of the four chairs, were cleaned with Dettol twice a day. Sometimes she even got up in the middle of the night to give them all another wipe.

Michael Docherty was setting the table for her as she prepared to serve up supper, opening the fridge to take out mayonnaise and ketchup. He had become such a regular visitor to the house, moving around the kitchen with all the ease of a man at home.

'The nerve of her!' Liza said, fuming. 'What right had she to come here like that! Just walking into my garden. Upsetting my son. Then leaving without even the decency to tell me where James is buried.'

'She's hurt,' Michael said.

'*I'm* hurt, Michael! I'm the one who has been left alone to fend for myself and Jamie without any help from James's money! She gets it all — that wife of his. And she doesn't deserve a penny of it. Her two children are grown up. They can fend for themselves now. And *she* has a job at NATO headquarters. James always said she cared more about her job than him.'

Michael hesitated. 'Liza … that was the truth, wasn't it? What you said he told you, that they had been separated for years?'

'Of course it's the truth. Why should I lie to you?' Liza marched over to the kitchen window and looked at Jamie playing in the garden. She knocked on the glass. 'Jamie … Jamie!'

'Shall I go and get him?' Michael offered.

'No.'

Liza knocked on the glass harder. 'Jamie. I will not call you again.'

Michael stood by the fridge watching as Liza took out a packet of paper napkins and placed one beside Jamie's mat on the table. Then she opened a cupboard and took out a small bottle, shaking out two tablets onto her palm and placing them on the napkin.

'Is he still reacting well to the drugs?' Michael asked.

Liza nodded, then a pause. 'Michael, I'm sorry I snapped. It's just … well, as I said, Düsseldorf is a big place. I'm sure there are many Catholic cemeteries there. But she didn't even have the decency to tell me where James was buried.'

'I know. But she's angry, Liza. She's looking for someone to blame.'

'So Jamie and I are to be her scapegoats, are we? Well I won't let her do that.'

Michael glanced back at Jamie in the garden, getting off his trike. 'Have you told him yet? About his dad?'

'No … not yet.' Liza walked to the window and stood looking at her son. 'That woman,' she said bitterly. 'I just hope she's proud of herself for what she has done to us.'

Later that evening, after Michael had left, Liza listened to Jamie's questions and knew the time had come to tell him about his father. She could not put it off any longer.

'Jamie,' she said at last, in a suppressed voice, 'I have something to tell you about Daddy.'

She told him the truth in a very simple way, because he was, after all, only five years old.

The tears she had expected did not come. Jamie looked back at her silently, not really comprehending. Just the same disappointed expression his face always wore whenever she told him Daddy had to go to Germany.

She looked at him carefully. 'Do you understand, Jamie?'

He nodded. 'Daddy's gone to Heaven.'

Later, while she was giving him his bath, drawing pictures on his soapy back with her finger, she gently asked him again. 'So you understand about Daddy, don't you, Jamie?'

'Yeah. He's gone to Heaven to see God. Draw another one, Mam.'

'Okay …' She drew on his back with her finger again. 'What's that?

'A load of elephants.'

'No.' Liza smiled. 'I only drew one. It's a horse.'

She rinsed water over his back. 'All right, out you get.'

'Just one more.' Jamie yawned. 'Do *two* horses this time.'

'No, You're tired out. Bed.'

She lifted him out and began towelling him down, feeling upset, as she did whenever she towelled him down, because of his thinness.

'Have you been eating your lunches?'

'Yeah — 'cept the carrots. I hate carrots.' He made a *'yukkk'* sound, then asked, 'Will Daddy get nice food to eat in Heaven?'

Liza was so taken by surprise, her eyes brimmed with tears. She quickly hugged Jamie to her to prevent him seeing her distress.

'I expect so, Jamie. I expect so.'

Jamie chuckled childishly. 'I hope they don't make him eat carrots!'


Liza awoke the next morning to find a shaft of bright sunlight streaming through a gap in the curtains. She turned baleful eyes towards it, then looked back at the clock — half-an-hour before her normal waking time.

Venetian blinds, that's what she needed, and what James had planned to buy for her. Venetian blinds for the window to keep the room nice and dark. The summer light always woke her too early.

She got out of bed and headed for the shower. Twenty minutes later she was down in the kitchen wiping over all the surfaces with anti-septic. Then she set the table for Jamie's breakfast, taking out a paper napkin and placing his tablets on it.

As usual, Jamie ignored all her calls. Even when she walked into his bedroom he refused to wake up from his blissful sleep. She walked over to the window and pulled back the curtains, standing for a moment to view the mountains in the distance.

'Jamie, come on, wake up. Your breakfast is on the table.'

'In a minute,' Jamie murmured, trying to stay asleep.

Liza stood looking down at his angelic face. She smiled and sat down on the bed, gently shaking him awake. 'Come on lazy bones. Rise and shi—'

Her face froze as Jamie opened his eyes. He looked at her, confused, recognising the panic in her face.

'Mam …?'

'It's all right. Everything's fine,' she said quickly, trying to smile. 'Come on. Get dressed now.'

Jamie looked reassured. He sat up and yawned, his thin arms stretched out.

Liza tried to swallow down her panic — the whites of Jamie's eyes were both blood red. He must have suffered a bleeding behind the eyes during his sleep.

'We've got games in school today,' he told her cheerily. 'Mr Docherty says we've got to play games to make our legs and arms strong.'

'No, you can't go to school today, Jamie.' Liza's hands were shaking as she reached for his clothes. 'It's your day for a check-up at the hospital. And we're late already, so come on, let's get you dressed and into the car.'

'What about my breakfast.'

'No time,' Liza replied shakily. 'They'll give you something to eat at the hospital.'


Two hours later, in the hospital's operating theatre, gowned nurses and doctors were gathered around the prone figure of Jamie as they performed an emergency Bone Marrow Aspirate.

Liza sat waiting in the corridor outside the ante-room, her face white, not even noticing when Michael Docherty sat down beside her.

'What's the latest?'

She turned her head slowly, looking at him glassily. 'Oh, I don't know anything yet. He's still …

in there.' She gestured to the operating theatre and looked away, staring ahead of her blankly.

'Liza …' Michael attempted to say some words of comfort to her, then changed his mind, deciding all he could do was stay with her, and wait with her, and be at her side when the doctors came out with their verdict.

When they did, it was Dr Brady who spoke to Liza, still wearing his surgical blues.

'The disease is back in the marrow. I'm very sorry.'

Liza suddenly slumped, all her strength seemed to be draining away. Michael caught her arm as the doctor continued in a calm, quiet voice.

'Our options are limited, I'm afraid. Jamie will have to go back on chemotherapy, but with relapsed AML … well, I have to be honest, the prognosis is not good. What Jamie really needs is a bone marrow transplant. But that is going to be difficult because he has no brothers or sisters, and we already know you are not a match.'

Liza felt the sudden tightening on her arm and knew instantly what Michael Docherty was silently saying to her … Jamie *did* have a brother and a sister — in Germany.

'Which is a pity,' Dr Brady continued. 'A donor from the family is often the best solution.'

Michael squeezed her arm again.

'No, no, *no* …' Liza shook her head at Michael. 'No, I will not ask that woman for anything.'

Michael could not believe her reaction. This was no time for pride! A child's life was at stake.

'Maybe you won't ask her,' Michael said fiercely, 'but I certainly will.'

A young hospital porter entered Maureen's office with a bouquet of beautiful flowers.

He grinned as he placed the flowers on the desk. 'You have an admirer, Maureen.'

Maureen stared at the bouquet, confounded. 'Who on earth …'

She reached for the small envelope, intrigued as she took out the card and read, *Your friend, Hans*.

'Hans!'

Andrea was stood by the desk, grinning. 'Well, well, things seems to be looking up for you at last, Maureen. Mind you, you'd better not tell Brian. He may not approve of a man sending his mother flowers.'

'That'd be the last straw,' Maureen agreed. 'He'd leave home for good.'

Maureen's eyes ranged over the flowers, they were really beautiful, and obviously very expensive. 'What do you think Hans is playing at — sending *me* flowers?'

'I think he fancies you,' Andrea said. 'I think he's fed up with fishing and wants to get his leg over.'

'Andrea, stop it!' Maureen giggled. 'You're wicked!'

The telephone started ringing.

'I bet that's him now,' Andrea said. 'Hello, Mau*reen*, did you like my flowers? ... Well, go on, answer it!'

Maureen reached for the phone, attempting to assume a business-like tone to her voice. 'Hello, Major Pinkerton's secretary ...'

'Mrs Lessing?'

The smile froze from Maureen's face as she recognised the voice of Michael Docherty. How *dare* he phone her here. How dare he phone her at all. Probably wanting some information for James's fancy-woman in Ireland. Well, she was finished with all that. She had too many other problems to care about.

'Mrs Lessing, I need to talk to you'

'I've already told you, Mr Docherty. Leave me and my family alone!' She slammed down the phone with a vengeance.

Andrea gaped. 'Who was that?'

'Nobody,' Maureen answered, her face red with anger. 'Nobody I want to talk about.'

# FOURTEEN

Maureen was alone in the house when the ringing of the telephone finally stopped and the answering-machine clicked on to Brian's message:

*Hello. Messages for the Lessing family after the tone please. Or try 383 4067 or mobile 1204 3689 ... BEEP.*

'Mrs Lessing. It's Michael Docherty again. I'm sorry but I have to explain to you about Jamie ...'

Maureen stood without movement as she listened to him explain. Her soul shrank within her as she realised what he was seeking from her.

' ... If they don't find a match, he'll die. It's a simple as that ... Mrs Lessing? ... Are you there, Mrs Lessing? I really need to talk to you.'

No, no, no, she could not do it, and would not do it. Maureen turned and walked out of the study, closing the door behind her, shutting out his voice and the terrible thing he was asking.

How dare he? After all that woman had taken from her — now he wanted her to allow one of her own children to suffer more pain — to have their bodies cut open and drained to help *that woman's* son.

She rushed back into the study to tell him '*No! That woman and her son are nothing to do with us! They are not our responsibility*!' But of course he was gone. Only his message remained on the tape of the answering machine. A message left for her to ponder over. A message to try and make her feel guilty. But, no, he would not succeed. She had nothing to feel guilty about. And she would not let her children be used in this way. It was not fair to them, and it was not fair to her. Nobody had bothered to inform her of the boy's birth — Liza Becker and James had sneakily colluded in keeping his existence a secret from her. So why should she be made to feel responsible for the boy now?

No, this was not her problem, and Michael Docherty had no right to try and make it so.

She put her finger on the *Erase* button of the answering machine and wiped the message from the tape.

As the night progressed, the telephone rang continually but Maureen refused to answer it, turning up the sound on the TV until it was almost blaring. She was very glad that both Maeve and Brian were out with friends tonight.

The next morning, a fax was waiting for her when she got into the office, the words brief and to the point: *Maureen, please ring me urgently. Hans Reiner*.

She rang Hans immediately.

'Maureen, I need to talk to you. Will you agree to have dinner with me this evening?'

She agreed, too weary to do otherwise. Why did everyone 'need to talk' to her all of a sudden?

As soon as she put down the phone she took a small bottle from her bag and helped herself to a 5mg tablet of Valium.

They sat at a table on the restaurant's terrace, overlooking the Rheinpromenade and river. Hans Reiner was making his selection from platters of seafood on the table, clearly enjoying every mouthful of his meal.

'Try the mushrooms in garlic,' he suggested. 'They are very delicious.'

Maureen tried the mushrooms in garlic, nodding her agreement. They really were delicious. But she had not come here solely for food.

'Hans, you said it was urgent.'

'What?'

'Your need to talk to me.'

'Oh, yes ...' Hans dabbed his lips with his napkin. 'Well, it's like this. The bank, unless we offer them something now, will call in the loan. Which means, of course, that you will have no choice but to sell the house. What they want is a lump sum now, or proof of an increase in your regular income.'

'And how am I supposed to do that? I'm facing redundancy, for God's sake.'

'I know, I know ...' Hans could not resist another forkful of mushrooms.

Maureen said, 'Do you know that Brian has got himself a part-time job?'

Hans nodded. 'He wants to help, I know.'

'He's been driving me mad lately, but all credit to him, he's doing his best. I even had to stop him selling off his old Volkswagen. Someone offered him a thousand marks for it.'

'You did right to stop him. He needs the car, and a thousand marks will not help. But I do have a suggestion that might work. We could argue that you did not know what you were signing.'

Maureen was puzzled by the ridiculousness of his suggestion. Or did he really think the bank would believe she was such a fool?

'Hans, we both know I'm legally responsible for the debt. The bank know it too.'

'They do know, yes. But we could embarrass them. "Financial Giant Forces Grieving Widow Out of Home." You threaten to go public. Banks hate bad publicity.'

'No!' Maureen cried sharply. 'Absolutely not! I'm not having my private business held up for public examination.'

Her raised voice drew the stares of diners at the surrounding tables.

Maureen smiled stiffly in apology to them, then excused herself and went to the Ladies' room and popped another Valium into her mouth.

Jesus Christ, she thought. How the bloody hell did I get into this mess? Seven weeks ago I had a happy life and a husband I loved and respected. Now where am I? Widowed and bankrupt and down in a Ladies' bog popping Valium ... Jesus Christ.

She returned to the table and gave Hans a small tight smile. 'I know your intentions are good, Hans, but credit me with some dignity. I'm not prepared to become some snivelling media tart for any amount of money. Not even to save my home. Besides, I'm not old enough — or young enough — to elicit any sort of sympathy from the crowd. I'm just a boring old middle-aged cliché and that's the truth of it. Now thanks for the dinner but I'm off. I'm a widow with a lot of weeds to sort out.'

She slung her bag on her shoulder and walked haughtily out of the restaurant, leaving Hans sitting open-mouthed behind her.

On the bus home, Maureen shrank back into herself and wondered why she had acted that way with Hans. It was unlike her to be so rude.

She had no idea that she was actually quite ill, her entire nervous system unstable, caused by the trauma of James's sudden death and the horrific shock of discovering his long-term adultery with another woman. If she could have challenged James, had it out with him in a series of screaming matches, or even been able to revile him to his face, it might have helped.

But James had escaped all retribution and responsibility for his actions, leaving only Liza

156

Becker for Maureen to focus her hatred on. A hatred that was making her slightly demented.

In that conclusion, Brian had been right. His mother needed help.

In Ireland, Father Cornelius was still praying for her, hoping she would receive the help of God.

# FIFTEEN

Liza Becker stood by the open door of the ante-room to the operating theatre, her face tense as she watched the anaesthetist checking the pulse monitor clipped onto Jamie's fingers.

Liza turned away.

She walked along corridors and downstairs until she finally sat to rest in the hospital chapel. It was small and sparse. Almost impersonal but for the tray of small thin candles flickering beside the altar.

Just like my Jamie, Liza thought. A small flame flickering through life. What had he done to suffer like this? How many more of these operations must he endure?

Inside the operating theatre, a masked nurse stood ready by the trolley of gleaming instruments as the surgeon made his first cut; then murmured, 'Nothing from the UK donor banks?'

Dr Brady answered negatively. 'No. It's an extremely unusual tissue type. We're trying Europe but it's not looking good.'

The surgeon glanced up as he handed a bloody scalpel back to the nurse. 'Does the mother know?'

'Not yet. We're still hoping for a donor.'

'Hmn … Wing and a prayer job, eh?'

Dr Brady's eyes were watching the surgeon's hands at work. 'Ready for the line?'

'Yes, ready.'

The nurse handed Dr Brady the plastic coil of Hickman line that was to be inserted into Jamie's chest. He unwound it and handed it to the surgeon who took it and leaned closer to the incision.

'Okay, nice and steady. Let's feed it in.'


Inside the hospital chapel, Liza's eyes were fixed on the candle-glow.

Nearly every one of those candles flickering before the altar had been lit by her.

A penny candle for Jamie.

Only now those penny candles cost ten-pennies. And she had lit five of them. One for each year of Jamie's life. And every year she had thanked God for the gift of him, because the doctors had told her at the beginning that his chance of life was slim.

But here he was, five years later, still fighting against all the odds. Still proving to the world what a brave little hero he was. And all because — and she was sure of this — every single day in the past five years his mother had gone into a church and lit a candle for Jamie.

The flame of the power of the Holy Spirit — never to be extinguished — lit by faith and kept burning by hope.

She stood up and turned away from the little altar and the candle-glow, her footsteps sounding loud in the empty chapel.

Outside the bustle and noise of the busy hospital assailed her; her short retreat into solitude was over.

A few corridors away from the Children's Oncology Ward, Michael Docherty stood by an open window, staring out over the sprawling hospital, inhaling deeply on a cigarette.

A moment later he hastily tossed the cigarette out of the window when he saw Liza coming round the corner of the corridor.

She gave him a cold look. 'This is a hospital you know.'

'Sorry, I'm nervous,' he said apologetically. 'It was the cigarette or a strong drink. I chose the lesser of the evils. So, how are you doing?'

'Better than you, by the look of things.'

'How's Jamie?'

'Still in theatre. His "line" should be in by now.'

'You didn't want to stay?'

'No, no, I prefer not to. It's …' Her voice trailed away.

'Liza.' Michael touched her arm.

'Let's walk,' she said.

'Okay.' Michael picked up a large carrier bag from the ground and fell into step beside her.

'You know, it's odd,' Liza said, 'but after a while this place begins to feel like a second home.'

'Yes, well, you've been coming here a long time.'

'I should have seen something …' she said with a frown. 'I should have seen it. But I really thought he was well.'

'We all did,' Michael agreed.

'I know I was paranoid about germs and Jamie catching anything, but I really thought it was gone for good.'

'What else could you do? You were getting on with your life, with Jamie's life.'

*And ruining his father's life,* Liza admitted to herself honestly. She kept her eyes fixed on the ground as she walked.

Then she lifted her eyes and looked at Michael with a woman-of-the-world directness. 'I just did what I had to do,' she said coldly.

Jamie groggily returned to consciousness as he was being wheeled into the Recovery Room.

'Mammy … where's Mam?'

The nurse bent down and smiled at him. 'It's all right, Jamie. She's on her way.'

Liza and Michael were walking along the corridor towards the recovery room.

'Oh, I forgot, I brought you something.' Michael opened the carrier bag and took out a huge handmade Get Well card, full of children's drawings and scrawled messages.

'The kids at school made it. Actually it's for Jamie, but you do make an appearance.' He pointed to a drawing of a small figure inside the card. 'Not very flattering I know, but the thought was there.'

Liza's heart was touched. 'Jamie will love it. Thanks. And you will thank the children, won't you?'

'Mrs Becker!'

Liza turned and shot forward when the nurse called her. 'He's fine,' the nurse smiled reassuringly. 'Just fine.'

'Oh, thank God.' Liza hurried into the Recovery Room and rushed over to Jamie on his stretcher.

'Hello, Jamie, hello … Look who's come to visit you? Mr Docherty. And he's brought you a huge *Get Well* card from all the children in school.'

'Yeah?' Jamie's groggy smile was full of surprise and delight. 'Did they, Mr Docherty? Did they make a card just for me?'

Michael Docherty could only smile and nod his head at the trusting child who was so full of innocence and everything good — nodding and shutting his teeth down on the emotion that engulfed him. Anyone with a heart would love Jamie.

Ten minutes later Michael was back on the hospital's payphone, calling Germany.

Maureen stood listening with strained attention to the voice on the answering machine.

'*Mrs Lessing. It's Michael Docherty. I just wondered if you'd had a chance to think about things yet. It's just that the situation is getting pretty critical here. Jamie has started back on the chemotherapy, he's had his Hickman line put in ...*'

Maureen's hand hovered over the receiver of the answerphone, propelled by an impulse to tell him how sorry she was for the boy. Really and genuinely sorry. God, she would feel sorry for any child who was that sick.

'*But they're still searching for a donor ... The problem is not only finding a donor, but finding the right match ... I understand this must be difficult for you, but, well, I need to talk to you about whether one or both of your children would —*'

'No!' She clicked off the machine and his voice, then she bent down and unplugged it, muttering vehemently to herself. 'So it's my *children* that Becker woman wants now, is it? Wants to use *my* children for the benefit of *her* son. First my husband, and now my kids! And you want to help her to get them. Well you can go to blazes, Michael Docherty, because that woman's getting nothing more from me!'

Maureen spent the evening at Andrea's house, the two of them chatting about everything but Maureen's problems.

163

'Are you bringing the kids to the barbecue?' Andrea asked.

'I might manage to drag Maeve along — by her hair.'

Andrea smiled, glancing over at a photograph of her own daughter. 'Teenagers — they think they're so bloody sophisticated.'

'Yeah,' Maureen agreed. 'The trouble is, they are.'

But no, that was not really true, Maureen thought, not her teenagers anyway. Maeve had only just turned fifteen, and in so many ways she was still just a kid, still needed to slide into bed beside her Mum when the world got too frightening. And Brian thought he was all grown up, but he was not. He was still insecure behind that veneer of arrogance and cynicism.

She suddenly thought of Hans Reiner, and his suggestion of threatening the bank to go public — how ridiculous! Not only would the public not give a damn about her own predicament — even her children were not young enough now to attract any kind of compassion.

'What about your new gentleman friend?' Andrea asked teasingly on the drive home. 'Perhaps you could bring *him* to the barbecue?'

'Andrea, please!' Maureen had to smile. 'Will you stop trying to matchmake me with every available man we know.'

'It's what happens when you get widowed or

divorced,' Andrea said knowingly. 'People do it all the time. Become your matchmaker. That's how I met my second husband and made my second big mistake.'

When Maureen entered the house, Maeve was speaking on the telephone, writing something down as she spoke.

'Yeah, I've got the number ... Yeah, Michael Docherty. Right, I'll tell her it's urgent ... No, I don't know if she got any of the messages, someone seems to have unplugged it — Oh hold on, this may be her ... Mum?'

Maeve turned her head and saw her mother standing there.

'Mum,' she whispered, putting her hand over the receiver. 'There's a man on the phone from Ireland. Michael Docherty. He says it's very urgent.'

Maureen walked forward, grabbed the receiver, slammed it down and then unplugged the hall telephone also.

'Mum!'

'You do not speak to that man again, do you hear me, Maeve! No matter how nice he may have sounded — he is not a friend! Not to you or Brian. And not to me.'

# SIXTEEN

In the Children's Oncology Ward, Michael Docherty stood by the door of a side room watching Jamie tucking into a lunch of pizza and chips, ignoring Mr Street, the Registrar, as he injected his line with Chemo.

Jamie was ignoring everyone, his eyes glued to the television as he chewed his pizza.

Typical kid! Michael thought, turning away to take a stroll down the corridor. He suddenly caught sight of Dr Brady and speeded his steps.

'Dr Brady!'

Dr Brady turned.

'Have you got a minute?' Michael asked. 'Please.'

Dr Brady gave him the minute, pleasantly at first, but then became increasingly uncomfortable at being questioned about such a delicate and private matter in the open thoroughfare of a hospital corridor.

'Mrs Becker is the boy's mother,' Dr Brady said with quiet sternness. 'And if she doesn't want to ask this woman for help, there is nothing I can do.'

'But you said there is a one-in-three chance of a sibling being a match?'

'No. We'd be looking at a Haplotyte mismatch at best.'

'Yes, but some kids have made it with that, yes?'

'Some have, yes.'

'So — isn't it worth a chance?'

Dr Brady sighed. 'Look, let's get something straight. I want to help the boy as much as you do. If I could force the mother to ask this woman for help, I would. But my hands are tied.'

'All right, I understand that. But what about Mrs Lessing? Could *you* not contact her and ask her?'

Astounded, Dr Brady replied, 'I am Jamie's doctor, Mr Docherty. I don't even know this other woman.'

'What does that matter?'

'There is such a thing as patient confidentiality. 'Which reminds me — are *you* a family member, Mr Docherty? Any relation to the boy or his mother?'

'Liza doesn't have any family. She moved here from Austria ten years ago.'

Dr Brady ignored this. 'No, you are not a family member. Does Mrs Becker even know you are speaking to me? No.'

Dr Brady smiled sourly.

'You are not God, Mr Docherty, and unfortunately neither am I. One look around this ward should tell you that.' He turned to go. 'Now please excuse me, I have work to do.'

Slowly, Michael walked back down the corridor,

167

frustrated and despondent. He reached Jamie's room just in time to witness Liza holding Jamie's head over a vomit bowl as he threw up his pizza lunch.

Having eaten no lunch himself, Michael drove back to St Mary's School in Bray just in time for his afternoon class.

Unable to concentrate, he sat in front of the class of six-year-olds and decided to read them a story.

'Okay, so this is a story about the Three Billy Goats Gruff and the wicked old Troll. Now, who knows what Trolls look like?'

A few hands went up.

'Donal. You tell us.'

'Trolls look just like me sister, sir.'

Michael ignored the laughter. 'What makes you say that, Donal?'

'Me Da, sir. He says me sister looks just like a trollop when she puts her lipstick on.'

Michael tried not to smile. 'Not quite the same thing. But, well, thank you for that, Donal. Now, anyone else ...?'

Dr Brady's conscience was disrupting his concentration as he found himself unable to forget his conversation with Michael Docherty. The situation was a difficult one ... but then leukaemia was a difficult disease ...

Yes, the man was right, he decided. If there was any chance at all to help Jamie, it was a chance that had to be grasped, and fast.

But how to do it?

An hour later, Liza entered and sat down in Dr Brady's office. A nurse stood close beside her, offering support as Dr Brady outlined the situation in a frank and calm voice.

'... With ninety-five per cent of Caucasian tissue types we would expect to find matches immediately. However, Jamie belongs to the other five per cent. So far, I'm afraid, it has been impossible to find a donor of the right type. And without a donor ...' he left the inevitable unsaid.

Liza refused to believe it. 'Have you tried everywhere?'

'Everywhere. The UK, Europe, America. All the major donor banks. It's very unfortunate, especially since we are well on the way to getting young Jamie back into remission again. But we are not giving up hope, Mrs Becker.'

Liza stared down at the bitten nails of her fingers. 'No, we must not give up hope.'

Dr Brady was watching her shrewdly. 'However,' he added. 'It might be worth looking at any other possible family members ... even a half-brother or half-sister, for instance, might possibly provide a suitable match ...'

It took a few seconds, through her shock, for Liza to realise that Dr Brady knew ... And only Michael

Docherty could have told him … Told Dr Brady and possibly even the entire hospital staff that she was not the respectable Mrs Becker they all thought she was, but that Jamie's father had been a married man with a wife and children back in Germany.

How *dare* he? How dare Michael take it upon himself to disclose her private business to anyone!

Michael was just leaving St Mary's School for the day when Liza stalked up to him in the empty playground.

'You told them,' she shouted. 'You had no right! None.'

'I'm sorry,' Michael said. 'But Jamie has rights too, doesn't he?'

'He's *my* son, Michael! It's him I'm trying to protect.'

'No, you're not.'

'What are you talking about?' She stared at him with shocked incredulity, slowly realising what he was implying. 'No! This isn't about me and her.'

'Isn't it?' he asked. 'It sure as hell isn't about Jamie — and he's the one that's suffering.'

'Do you think I don't know that?'

'I know you're angry. I know you'll never swallow your pride. For Christ's sake, Liza …'

'Look, Michael,' she said in a more reasonable tone, 'I know you're trying to help … but please stop trying to run my life.'

He nodded. 'Okay. I'm sorry. I honestly thought I was trying to save one.'

He left Liza staring after him.

She caught up with him as he about to get into his car. 'Michael!'

He turned slowly, his expression cool.

'All right,' Liza cried. 'If she wants me to beg, then I will. But will you do it, Michael? Will you ask her? I'm … I'm just frightened she'll say no.'

Or refuse to even discuss it, Michael thought, recalling all his ignored telephone messages.

'I'll ask her,' he said.

'Thanks.' Liza took a breath. 'You're a good man, Michael.'

'Yeah.' He smiled. 'For an ex-alcoholic.'

'You never really liked James, did you?'

Michael shrugged. 'I never really knew him. I always got the impression he was a bit wary of me. But can I ask you something?'

'What?'

He looked at her, genuinely puzzled. 'All those lies he told you. Year after year. All those missed birthdays and Christmasses because he had to "work". You must have suspected something?'

Liza turned away from his eyes, unable to look at him. 'Oh, I don't know … He had his children to support — she wouldn't let him go, that's what he said.'

'But now we know that wasn't true, none of it. So

imagine how his wife must feel? Twenty-two years is a long time.'

Liza looked pensive. 'His wife, yes. And his children. Do you think they hate me?'

'I don't know, Liza. I honestly don't.'

'I do,' Liza said, turning away.


It was still early evening when Michael Docherty drove towards the Mullens B&B hotel in Dublin.

It was pointless for him to ring Germany again, he had decided. Maureen Lessing clearly regarded him as an enemy on the other side. She would never believe that the only side he was on was Jamie's.

So Jamie's side had to be put to Maureen Lessing by someone else. Someone she trusted as a true and genuine friend. And the only place where Michael knew he might find such a friend was at the Mullens.


Bridget Mullen was perched on top of a stepladder when Michael brought his car to a stop outside the house.

She was dead-heading the flowers in the hanging baskets, calling over her shoulder to the open doorway, 'Sean! Hand me up the watering can, will you? Sean! Where are you?'

Michael got out of the car and walked up to the house.

Bridget shouted even louder. 'Sean!'

'There you go. Is this what you want?' Michael held up the watering can.

Bridget jerked around, ignoring the offered can, staring at him in slow recognition. 'Well, my God ... Maureen's not here.'

'I know.'

'She's back in Germany.'

'I know.'

'So who is it you're here to see then?'

'Sean.'


'Jesus,' said Sean softly, after listening to Michael Docherty's account of the situation.

'The bottom line is,' Michael continued, 'without a bone marrow donor Jamie will die, and it looks like our only real hope of finding one is within the Lessing family.'

Only Sean and Nora sat with Michael Docherty in the lounge. Bridget had been left in the kitchen and told to stay there.

'It's as simple as that,' Michael said.

Nora shot a worried glance over at Sean for his reaction. He steadfastly ignored her, refusing to even look at her.

Sean cleared his throat and looked solemn. When he eventually spoke his voice was very tight. 'You do realise,' he said, 'that this is the first I've heard of any of this.'

Michael glanced at Nora. 'I'm sorry it was necessary for me to have to tell you anything.'

'So, how can we help?' Sean asked.

'We urgently need to trace James Lessing's nearest family. To test them.'

Sean still didn't quite understand the difficulty. 'His nearest family? Well they're going to be in Germany. Maureen's kids.'

'Mrs Lessing has refused to help.'

Sean sat back, initially appalled, then quickly realising the emotional complications of the situation.

Nora sprang to Maureen's defence, glaring at Michael Docherty. 'The way you talk anyone would think Maureen had no *right* at all to consider her own children first. Look, does Maureen know that you're here talking to us?'

'No.'

Nora glanced over at Sean.

Michael said, 'She won't talk to me. That's why I came to you.'

A long silence followed.

Later that night, in Nora and Sean's bedroom, the atmosphere was extremely tense. Sean's manner was chilly and resentful.

'You should have told me.'

'She's my best friend, Sean.'

'Your best friend — I thought that was me.'

174

'You're my husband, Sean. It's different.'

Sean stopped unbuttoning his shirt and gave her a look. 'Yeah, so I'm learning.'

Nora pulled back the duvet and got into bed. 'Look, I'd have told you if I could. She was desperate. She didn't want anyone to know. How would you feel? Five years. Five years or more and all that time he had another woman and son in Ireland, the bastard.'

'Yeah, yeah, I know all that.'

'But you don't *understand*, do you?' Nora retorted angrily. 'What it must feel like! To know that the two of them were conniving behind her back like that, and for so long. She feels ashamed, betrayed. They made a fool of her and left her bankrupt into the bargain. And right now she's all messed up in her head. She's needs our help, Sean.'

'Ours?' Sean gave her an exaggerated gape. 'Oh, so it's "our" help she needs now, is it?'

'Alright, alright, I'm sorry, I should have told you.'

Sean got into bed, calmer, his face thoughtful. 'You know,' he said quietly, 'when you think of the circumstances, this is a pretty stupid argument.'

Nora nodded. 'What are we going to do?'

'God knows ... Someone has to talk to Maureen.'

'Sean, I can't take sides against her.'

'No. And you can't stand by and let that kid die either.'

Ten minutes later, Sean spoke again, breaking the long silence.

'Perhaps I'm not a clever man, and maybe I do have a slow way of thinking about things, but I've never lacked good, practical, common sense.'

Nora looked at him, bewildered. 'So?'

'So my common sense tells me that the longer you put this thing off, the harder it's going to be. For both of us.'

Nora could no longer disagree with him. The situation was awful but she couldn't just stand by and do nothing. 'You're right,' she said. 'I'll phone Maureen now.'

'Good girl.' Sean lifted the telephone off his side-cabinet and placed it on the bed between them. 'Have you her number in your head?'

'No, it's in my book, downstairs. I'll have to go down and get it.'

'And lose your nerve? No, just lift up the phone there and ask Directory Enquiries to give you her number.'

Nora did so, and then dialled the number in Germany ... 'Hello, Maureen, it's Nora, sorry to call so late, but we've had a visitor here ...'

Sean watched his wife, tense and pink-faced as she attempted to convey to Maureen what Michael Docherty had said. The response from the other end was so agitated, and so loud with anger, Sean didn't even have to lean closer to hear.

'*It's emotional blackmail, Nora. I don't care what*

176

*Michael Docherty says. He's not a doctor. He's a lackey of that Becker woman. It's not my responsibility, Nora. My responsibility is to my own children ...'*

When Nora eventually put down the phone, her face was pallid and upset. Sean stroked her arm, by way of comfort.

'Do you know who I blame?' Nora blurted angrily. 'That bloody deceitful husband of hers. He's the one who's really responsible for all this!'

# SEVENTEEN

Two nights later, Nora had a firmer grip on herself as she looked at Michael Docherty standing on the doorstep. Her hand resting on the door jamb told him he was not going to be invited in.

'... I did my best. I'm sorry.'

'Could you, maybe, talk to the children themselves? The older one. The son?'

'No!' Nora shook her head with indignation. 'I can't ... I won't go behind Maureen's back.'

'Mrs Mullen'

'No. I've tried. I'm sorry.' Nora shut the door with finality.


Liza Becker was still scrubbing and cleaning and sterilising.

In the hospital, Michael found her in the small kitchen used primarily by the families of transplant patients. The kitchen was already spotlessly clean, with labelled cupboards for the individual families. Michael moved over to the window and stood for a time staring out at the darkness of the night.

'Did you speak to her? Liza asked.

'No.'

'So you haven't asked her yet?'

Michael turned and looked at her, unable to tell her.

'So *when* will you ask her, Michael?'

'I'm …' Michael cleared his throat. 'I'm going to phone her later tonight. As soon as I get home.'

'Good.' Liza nodded, then continued scrubbing and scrubbing at the already spotless work surface in front of her, her head lowered.

Michael turned and silently strode out, down along the corridor to the Oncology ward.

In the semi-lit darkness of the ward, he paused in the doorway and stared across at Jamie's bed, a small figure fast asleep. He would have looked normal, just young Jamie asleep in his bed; but now there was a difference — because Jamie had lost all his hair.

Michael stood for a time just staring at Jamie's small bald head … then turned and walked away.


When he returned home, he did not phone Maureen Lessing. He phoned Aer Lingus instead, booking himself a seat on the following morning's 5.20 a.m. flight to Düsseldorf.

# EIGHTEEN

'It's their egos, you see?'

Andrea laughed as she locked the door of the Volkswagen and walked with Maureen towards the front entrance of the JHQ hospital.

'You tell them you're not looking for a long-term relationship and they start getting all precious. "*But don't you like me?*" I mean what a stupid bloody question. If I didn't like him I wouldn't have slept with him in the first place, would I?'

Maureen didn't answer.

Andrea nudged her. 'Hey, this is my sex life we're talking about.'

'I know and I'm listening.' Maureen smiled. 'He's a Registrar, isn't he?'

'Yeah.' Andrea grinned. 'Nice healing hands. I'll introduce you to him at the barbecue. No excuses — you're coming.'

'Mrs Lessing?'

Maureen turned, completely stunned to see Michael Docherty approaching her.

'Can I speak to you, Mrs Lessing?'


They sat at a window table in the hospital canteen.

Maureen's coffee remained untouched in front of her.

'Whatever you may feel about Liza,' he said, 'her son is completely innocent.'

Maureen regarded him stonily. 'So am I the one on trial here?'

'No one is accusing you —'

'That's very generous of you. Nevertheless, you still just turn up here, after harassing me constantly with phone calls, recruiting my friends to do likewise.'

'Mrs Lessing. He's five years old … just a kid.'

'And how many times must I tell you that he is not *my* responsibility. I have my own family.'

'Then surely you must understand how she feels? He is her only child. Jamie is her life. She's not some… Look, Liza is an educated, cultured woman. Ten years ago she came to Ireland on a Student Exchange Programme, fell in love with the country and the life, and stayed.'

Maureen's expression was wry. 'You make it sound terribly romantic.'

'Everyone has a dream.' He shrugged. 'Isn't that why you came to Germany?'

'I came to Germany to be near my husband and his work. Now I find I'd have been better off staying at home in Ireland. Since that's where he seems to have spent most of his time.'

Michael could not deny her grievance or the

injustice of it. 'I understand your anger, Mrs Lessing. But you are angry with the wrong person. He lied to Liza too.'

Maureen chortled sarcastically. 'Don't make me laugh!'

This was not the issue. Michael wanted to avoid this. He wanted to talk to her only about Jamie.

'She got pregnant —'

'By my husband.'

'Had the baby she'd always longed for, and she thought her life was perfect —'

'Without giving a damn or a care about his wife and two other children in Germany?'

'Jamie was diagnosed with leukaemia. It was the day before his first birthday. He spent it in St Jude's Hospital in Dublin.'

Maureen suddenly pushed back her chair. 'I'm late. I have to go.'


Liza was still scrubbing away in the kitchen when Michael returned to the hospital that night. This time she had turned her attention to the sink.

Liza looked up. 'I rang the school ... they said you had taken the day off ... gone to Germany.'

Michael nodded.

The temperature in the kitchen was unbearably hot.

'Did you tell her?'

Michael's eyes were puffy with tiredness. He had not been to bed the night before.

'Yes, I told her,' he said quietly. 'But as no one told her anything during the past five years, she's not prepared to listen to anything now.'

On Sunday afternoon, Andrea's barbecue was well-attended.

Chickens roasted on a spit. Trestle tables were laden with food, barrels of beer quickly emptying. She had even hired a small band to add to the festive air.

After a conversation with Major Pinkerton, Maureen walked across the garden to where Maeve was standing near the barbecue, holding a paper plate full of food, and looking totally bored.

'Can we go soon?'

'Maeve. Come on, it's a party.'

Maeve looked around at all the guests — not one under twenty. She said sneeringly, 'You could have fooled me. Christ, warm beer, crap music and chicken legs. I hate chicken. And why wasn't Brian forced to come? No, he can do what he likes, can't he.'

'Maeve, please —'

Andrea appeared from nowhere, a sly grin on her face and a bottle of wine in each hand. 'So what do you think?'

Maureen nodded her head enthusiastically. 'Oh, uh, it's great. Fabulous party, Andrea.' She held up her plate. 'And the chicken's delicious.'

'Screw the chicken — I meant *him*.' Andrea indicated towards a bearded young man in his thirties, wearing an apron and chef's hat, slaving away over the barbecue.

'Is that him, your Registrar?'

'That's Manfred. He reckons the beard gives him gravitas, but all it gives me is a rash.' She giggled. 'He works in Paediatric Oncology. I'll introduce you to him in a minute.' Andrea moved off, waving her bottle of wine at another guest.

*Paediatric Oncology.* The words hit Maureen like a blow. Was there no escape? Was Andrea in on the conspiracy to torment her? Had Michael Docherty recruited her too …

Suddenly it all became too much for her, the full weight and misery of her life, widowhood, bankruptcy, the shocking discovery of her husband's disloyalty and deceitful betrayal, and now his fancy-woman had got her lackey to come over here to Germany to harass her at her place of work — was there to be no end to the violations inflicted by that woman?

Maureen stood for a moment looking around at all the smiling and happy faces of the people at the party and suddenly felt deadeningly tired and sick of everything … Her eyes welled with tears … big, bubbling, bursting tears …

'Mum!' Maeve exclaimed. 'Christ, Mum, what's wrong?'

'Let's go,' she mumbled to Maeve, then hurried

across the lawn away from the crowd and the strain of it all. She would apologise to Andrea tomorrow, but now she just wanted the privacy of her own home.

Strangely, the person she turned to for comfort was Brian. She was sitting at the kitchen table in her dressing-gown later that night, waiting for him when he came home from his part-time job in the student bar.

'How was work?' she asked.

'Okay. I'm getting the hang of it.' He sniffed his T-shirt. 'God, this stinks of beer.' He pulled it off, poured himself a large tumbler of water, and sat down at the table.

'So, how was the barbecue?'

'A great success for Andrea, A disaster for me …'

She told Brian everything, about Liza Becker's son and his illness. The telephone messages left on the machine by Michael Docherty. The call from Nora. Then Michael Docherty's arrival in German. The pressure and harassment and emotional blackmail of it all.

She was so upset, Brian was moved to reach out and awkwardly put an arm around her shoulder.

'I didn't want to tell you,' she said.

'I'm glad you did. We're a family, Mum. We shouldn't have secrets.'

'Someone should have told that to your father.' Maureen wiped her eyes. 'This situation is the result of *his* actions — but it seems I'm the one who's expected to deal with it.'

Brian still couldn't take her bitterness against his father. He stood up and poured himself more water.

'Look,' he said, 'you have enough on your plate with all the problems here, without being upset and harassed by some stranger from Ireland. I'll speak to this Michael Docherty character myself. Tell him to get lost. Warn him off. Alright?'

Maureen nodded in agreement. 'I'm glad I told you, Brian. I just didn't know what else to do. It all came to a head today at the barbecue. And Maeve ... she must think I'm mad.' She quickly looked up at Brian. 'I've told Maeve nothing about any of this.'

'Don't worry about Maeve, Mum, she'll understand. I'll talk to her.'

'No. No, don't, Brian. Let me tell her. Please. I want to choose my time, and then explain it all to her very carefully, gently. I don't want you to say anything to her about the boy being ill, not yet.'

'Okay, don't worry.' Brian bent and took hold of her arm. 'Come on, go up to bed, Mum. You look worn out.'

'A little peace,' Maureen agreed, standing up. 'A little peace of mind and a good night's sleep in which I don't dream. That's what I need. Goodnight, love.'

'Night, Mum.'

Brian watched his mother leave the kitchen and knew he had to help her with this. First thing in the morning he would telephone Michael Docherty and tell him to mind his own business and leave the Lessing family alone. But right now he could do something else — he could make sure that Maeve didn't throw a wobbly and go all sentimental about her sick little 'half-brother' in Ireland — making it all even harder for Mum.

Oh sure, his mother had asked him to say nothing to Maeve, but she wasn't thinking straight right now, was she? It was up to him, her son, to help her. Who else did she have now Dad was gone?

Brian pulled a clean T-shirt from the ironing basket, pulled it on, then walked down the hall into the living room and over to the television — it was blaring. Maeve had not heard him come into the room or even the house.

He switched the TV off.

'Hey!' Maeve sat up and glared. 'Turn that back on! It's the video of *L.A. Confidential* for Christ's sake!'

'Then you can rewind and watch it tomorrow,' Brian replied, bending to turn off the video recorder. 'Anyway, that film's too grown-up for you.'

For a second Maeve was stunned into silence — seeing a flash of her father in Brian — the same face, the same dominance in the voice.

'Mum got very upset at the barbecue today, didn't she?' Brian said.

'Yeah, she did.'

'Do you know why?'

'No. She just mumbled something about feeling tired and sick.'

Brian then told Maeve the reason for his mother's upset, and why all communication with Michael Docherty, Nora and Sean Mullen, and anyone else in Ireland, must be broken.

Maeve's eyes popped in astonished disbelief.

'These phone calls demanding the supply of a donor have got to stop,' Brian said. 'The boy's illness is not our responsibility.'

'And that's it?'

'It's a family decision,' Brian said.

'Is it? So how come nobody discussed it with me?'

'We're discussing it now.'

'Bullshit. You and Mum have already agreed.'

'Keep your voice down.'

Maeve lowered her voice, but she was still very angry. 'If he's sick we should help him. He's our half-brother.'

'Says who?'

Maeve sat back, appalled at his callousness. 'Oh, come on, Brian, I know you thought the sun shone out of Dad's arse, but get real.'

Brian's eyes flashed. 'Hey, fuck you —'

'You weren't his only son, Brian. That's what you don't want to believe, isn't it?' Maeve jumped to her feet. 'So why don't you go to Ireland and see for yourself. But no, you're scared to go, aren't you?

Scared shitless of what you might find out about your precious father. But I've been to Ireland and I've seen photographs of him — of *my* half-brother. And if I want to help him, I will!'

'What's going on?' Maureen stood in the doorway.

Maeve turned on her witheringly. 'Thanks, Mum … Thanks for nothing.'

Utterly dismayed, Maureen stared at Brian, knowing what he had done. 'Brian, I asked you —'

'What did you ask him?' Maeve demanded. 'Not to tell *me*?'

Maureen sighed, 'Maeve, listen to me …'

'No!' Maeve was fuming and hissing like a mad young alley cat. 'I'm not listening to you because I know more than you think I do! I heard you on the phone, to Nora, refusing to help!' She pointed at Brian. 'And then you go and tell that ass and not me.'

'Oh, grow up,' Brian said. 'That's pathetic.'

'Pathetic!' Tears were filling in Maeve's eyes. 'He's only five years old and you are going to let him die.' She wheeled on her mother. 'I know what *you're* doing. You're punishing him for being Dad's son!'

She slammed out.

Brian stood there in the awful silence, feeling his sister's accusation.

The next day, in her break at the hospital, Maureen

found herself compelled to take a walk down to the Paediatric Oncology ward. She heard childish laughter and noise even before she reached the glass-panelled window of the ward door.

At the door, she stood to look through the glass panel and see what all the unexpected laughter was about … a group of young bald-headed kids on Chemo pumps were enjoying having their faces painted … laughing as a nurse had her face painted too.

A great sob swelled up in Maureen's throat, and only then did she understand why she had been weeping the day before. She knew — she *knew* all about Chemo kids — and yet she had allowed herself to turn her back on one of those children in a blind defiance of the past. Allowed her own dark resentment and hatred to black out her soul.

A rise of sudden laughter brought her eyes back to the children — the blue paint on the nurse's face delighted them.

Closer, closer she peered through the glass at the painted blue faces of the group of young brave hearts and their nurses, all fighting the illness, conquering the nausea, and all hoping for the match of a donor.


Many of the teenage students had already piled out of the gates and were on their way home when Maureen reached the International School.

She paused, and looked beyond the gates, thinking for a minute that she had missed Maeve.

She stood, disappointed, because after the row last night Maeve would probably be gone to one of her friends' houses and stay there till late.

As she turned to go, she saw Maeve lounging against a wall across from the school, in the company of a teenage lad, both in uniform, and both smoking cigarettes.

Maeve did a good job of hiding her surprise when her mother approached her. 'I can find my own way home,' she said flatly. 'I do know where the bus stop is.'

Maureen ignored the cigarette that Maeve defiantly continued to smoke.

'I know you do. But I left work early today. I just thought we might go somewhere for a coffee.'

Maeve took a long drag on her cigarette and gave no response. She tossed away the cigarette and began to walk, glancing back coldly at her mother. 'Why did you come?'

'I want to talk to you, Maeve.'

'No lectures, please. Not here.'

'No, no lectures.'

'What then? You don't usually waste time meeting *me* for a coffee.'

'No, but I went to the Paediatric Oncology ward today, and I've been thinking ... about Jamie. If you really do want to help him. If you want to test as a donor ...'

Maeve's expression was incredulous as she stopped and slowly turned to face her mother.

Maureen could hear the excitement in Michael Docherty's voice on the other end of the line. She had explained it all carefully to him. Finally, she added just two conditions.

'I don't want Jamie to know who Maeve is. And secondly, I don't want any meetings, or any connection whatever, between us and the boy's mother. Understand?'

'*Yes. Yes of course, I understand. And thank you …*'

'Don't thank me,' Maureen replied. 'It wasn't my decision. I just allowed Maeve to make her own.'

She replaced the receiver, turning to see Brian standing obdurate in the kitchen doorway.

'I want no part of this,' Brian said.

'Okay.'

'You're letting that Becker woman win again, you know that?

'Maybe. But sometimes in life you have to learn how to lose.'

'I want no part of it. None whatsoever.'

'If that's your decision, Brian.'

'It certainly is.'

Brian turned and strode to the study, slamming the door behind him.

Three mornings later, Liza Becker was sitting alone

in the front pew of the hospital chapel when Michael Docherty slipped in and sat down beside her.

She looked at him. 'Well?'

He nodded. 'The results of the preliminary blood tests are hopeful. Dr Brady has asked them to come over to Ireland so some further tests can be done here.'

Liza's relief was palpable. 'Oh, thank God.'

'To be honest,' Michael said seriously, 'I'm not sure God had a lot to do with it.'

Liza smiled, but without reproach. 'It's so easy for you to be cynical, Michael.'

'Force of habit.'

'When are they coming?'

'They're going to try and get a flight out this afternoon. But the results,' Michael added cautiously, 'they're only "hopeful". So don't expect too much, will you?'

# NINETEEN

On the aircraft, Maureen explained to Maeve, 'That day, after I had visited the oncology ward, I made inquiries about whether I could personally help the boy, but I was told no. To register as a donor for a bone marrow transplant, you have to be no more than forty years old. Oh, you can donate up to the age of fifty-five, but the first time you can't be more than forty.'

'But what good would *you* have been?' Maeve exclaimed. '*You* have no blood connection to Jamie.'

'There was that aspect to consider also,' Maureen agreed. 'But you know, Maeve, not *all* bone marrow donors are relatives of the patient. That's why there are donor banks all over the world. Sometimes a person living thousands of miles away can turn out to be a match.'

'But not in Jamie's case,' Maeve said, slightly annoyed at her mother for taking away from the grandness of her noble gesture. 'Jamie is a special case.'

'Yes, and I believe the doctors at the hospital in Dublin think that too — in Jamie's case, his only hope is dependent on a family relative with the right tissue type.'

'And that's me,' Maeve said proudly. 'Because whether you like it or not, Mum, I *am* his half-sister.'

*Ladies and Gentlemen, welcome to Dublin. Thank you for flying with Aer Lingus. We hope you have enjoyed your flight and that we will see you on board again soon.*

'Well, here we are,' Maeve exclaimed excitedly. 'Back in dear old Dub.'

Sean and Nora were waiting for them at the airport, where Nora embraced Maureen in a number of tight hugs, each one more apologetic than the hug before, gazing anxiously into Maureen's eyes. 'Are you *sure* you're okay about this?' she asked repeatedly.

'I'm fine, Nora. It was Maeve's decision. I'm just here as her chaperone.'

Sean Mullen, strangely for him, also gave Maureen a quick hug with a sad, half-hidden smile on his face. 'You know you are doing the right thing,' he said simply.

'Ahem … excuse me?' Maeve interjected, shifting her weight from one foot to the other and looking deflated. 'Is no one going to say hello to *me*?'

'Ah! Now *here's* our star!' Sean cried, grabbing Maeve in a bear-hug. 'Someone told me there's a load of men in white coats waiting for you! So come on.' He lifted her bag and held her hand and led her out of the airport to the front seat of his waiting taxi.

When Maureen and Nora were seated in the

back, Sean looked at Maeve beside him and smiled, 'Straight to the hospital, Miss Lessing?'

Maeve nodded. 'Straight on, Mr Mullen.'

Nora whispered to Maureen, 'What time is your appointment?'

'No particular time. They said to just get there as quickly as we could.'


Maeve and Maureen sat opposite Dr Brady as he explained what becoming a donor actually entailed.

'The transplant procedure itself is relatively simple. The marrow is extracted by a hollow needle inserted into the back of your hip bone. The marrow is then cleaned and fed to the patient as an infusion through the Hickman line ...'

When he had concluded, Maureen was looking less worried, but Maeve seemed disappointed by the simplicity of it all.

Then Dr Brady clarified the real problem they all faced.

'The preliminary blood typing seems to indicate a four antigen Haplotype mismatch.'

Maeve didn't understand. 'Is that bad?'

'It's larger than we would normally like. That's why we need to do some further tests.'

'And then if everything is okay?'

'We would do the transplant tomorrow.'

'Will Jamie be in the operating room with me?'

'Oh, no, no. Our patients generally never meet their donors.'

Maeve could barely hide her disappointment … none of this was turning out to be quite the romantic gesture she saw it as — a brother and sister lying side by side in the operating theatre, two siblings who had never met … And then in later years, the truth, when Jamie discovered who he owed his life to …

'Of course, they *can* meet, if they wish,' Dr Brady added. 'But it is not usual. However, in this case, I think we will leave that decision to the two families.'

Maureen replied stonily, 'Maeve *is* aware of all the circumstances, Doctor.'

'Right. Then let's get started.'


Maeve was grinning widely as she waited for the nurse to take her blood samples.

The nurse glanced over at her, perplexed, 'Are you all right there?'

'Oh, I'm all right,' Maeve replied. 'It's Mum you should be worrying about.'

Maureen, looking very concerned, was staring down at the tray of vacuum phials and needles laid out for use.

'Are *you* all right, Mrs Lessing?'

'No, I'm not.' Maureen shook her head. 'I'll sit this one out if you don't mind.' She squeezed Maeve's hand. 'I'll see you later.'

After she had quickly left the room, Maeve laughed at the nurse. 'You'd never believe she worked in a hospital, would you?'

'Oh I'm the same. Faint at the first sight of blood — especially my own,' the nurse joked; then added, 'Seriously, though, I have a little girl myself, so I know how she feels. We mothers can take any amount of pain ourselves, but we cringe at the slightest pin-prick into our children.'

'Hey!' Maeve exclaimed indignantly. 'I'm not a little girl. I'm fifteen!'

Jamie had lost a lot of his energy. He played listlessly with his Gameboy, ignoring his untouched tea-tray on the locker beside him.

Liza spoke to him anxiously. 'Come on, Jamie, you haven't eaten anything. Please, for me. You have to eat.'

'My mouth hurts.'

'How about if I go and get you some ice cream? Will you eat that?'

Jamie nodded without looking at her, and continued playing his Gameboy.

'But will you *eat* the ice cream, Jamie?'

'Yeah.'

'Good boy.'

Liza gathered up her purse and headed for the Tea Bar.

The Tea Bar was situated close to one of the Adult Outpatient Clinics, serving both patients and hospital staff. A large room with an open-plan area for seating, and very busy.

Maureen paid for her tea and began to make her way back through the throng to find an empty table.

She suddenly stopped … Liza Becker was standing less than ten feet away, in the queue, purse in hand, staring at her in recognition.

Liza suddenly stepped towards her, as if to speak.

Maureen stepped back — holding up her palm in a signal for Liza to keep away from her — uttering only one word.

'Don't.'

Liza glanced nervously and self-consciously around her at the people waiting to be served, and Maureen put down her tea on a nearby table and walked out of the room.

# TWENTY

Maeve was truly proud of herself. She had not flinched once during the blood tests, and the transplant was due to take place the following day.

Returning to the Mullens' house, Jenny and Niamh had decided to welcome Maeve back to 'dear old Dub' with an invitation to join them on a night out in Temple Bar.

'The Cranberries are doing a one-night gig there,' Jenny said. 'You like them, don't you?'

'Yeah, great … I mean *great* great!' Maeve responded with delighted starry eyes. 'The Cranberries are still really big in Germany.'

Sean, having been given the job of driving the girls into town, was totally unimpressed by their excitement.

'Now, I'm not a man who likes to brag,' he declared boastfully, 'but when *I* had my own band …'

Jenny and Niamh groaned as he launched into a long monologue about his own days as a rock star in the early Seventies.

'… Course in those days we were considered "new wave" too. All the bands were. Captain Beefheart. King Crimson …'

'They were ahead of their time,' Jenny giggled.

Niamh nudged Maeve wickedly. 'He's still got his crushed velvet loons, haven't you, Da?'

'Too right I have. And me Afghan coat.'

The giggling in the back seat was becoming convulsive.

'At least we *looked* good,' Sean continued. 'Not like this Cranberries lot you're going to see.'

At Temple Bar the girls piled out of the Espace with relief and excitement. 'Right,' said Sean. 'I'll meet yous back here at eleven. And you,' he directed a look of stern warning at Maeve. 'Don't be late. You've got a big day tomorrow.'


In the bathroom of the oncology ward, Liza and Jamie were also getting prepared for the big day.

Jamie sat in the bath, listening to her telling him all the exciting details as she leaned over and adjusted the special string-vest that protected and covered his Hickman line.

'And I get my own room? Just for me only?'

'Yes. It's called an "isolation" room.'

'With a television and a video and everything?'

'Yep, *and* your own remote control.'

'Wow. Cool.'

Liza smiled. 'Good, huh? You can even choose your own videos.'

'Yeah, but ...' Jamie's excitement suddenly faded. He looked up at her with grave seriousness.

'You won't tell my mates at school, will you? About my donor being a *girl*, will you?'

Liza laughed out loud … and began washing his hair.


Back at the Mullens' house, Bridget was already in her dressing-gown, pouring out a cup of tea for Nora and Maureen, and a cup for herself to take up to bed.

'Now,' she said with finality, 'yous have your tea, and everything's locked up, so I'm away to my bed. Goodnight.'

Maureen smiled. 'Goodnight, Bridget.'

'Night,' said Nora.

Bridget stopped in her tracks and looked at Nora. 'Your man in number seven was complaining about the hot water being too hot. Bloody ridiculous. Tell Sean.'

'I will, Bridget.'

'Oh, and you, Maureen — I nearly forgot. Your "friend" from Bray was on the phone looking for you.'

'Who? Michael Docherty?'

'That's the one. Says he'll phone you the minute he gets any news.'

'Oh, right.'

Bridget turned to go, a disgusted tone in her voice. 'The hot water was too hot, indeed? Tourists

… what are they like? Next they'll be saying the cold water is too cold.'

Nora and Maureen looked at each other and grinned. 'You ought to see her on a full moon,' Nora said. 'Listen, about me phoning like that. I didn't want to interfere.'

'I know. Forget it.' Maureen's smile was forgiving. 'Besides, it made a change from all my problems with the bank.'

'Maureen, if you need money —'

'No, not at all. Nora, I was only joking. Honestly. You and Sean have done enough already.'

'Sean wants to help. We both do. But listen now, about Bridget …' Nora lowered her voice. 'We haven't told Bridget or the girls anything about anything, okay? Bridget means well, but she would only fret. And that's all you need right now with this transplant coming up.'

'I hope we're doing the right thing,' Maureen murmured.

'You are. It's a matter of life or death now. You couldn't really do anything else.'

Maureen nodded. 'I just wish Brian agreed with you.'

# TWENTY-ONE

The Student Bar at the Heinrich Heine College in Düsseldorf was crowded: cigarette smoke, music and noise filled the air. Eva pushed her way through the crowd, followed by a lively group of her friends.

About to order drinks, Eva faltered — surprised to see Brian serving behind the bar. They had not seen each other since the night she had stormed out of his house. She had not gone running back to him as he had expected. And since then, she had steadfastly refused to return any of his telephone calls.

Eva's expression and voice were cool. 'What's this then, Brian? A new career move?'

Brian shrugged. 'It helps with the course fees.'

'So, how's your Mum?'

'Same as usual.' He gave her an accusing look. 'When am I going to see you again?'

Eva's cool facade seemed to crumble for a moment. She bit her lip, unable to look at him. 'Brian … I don't know how to say this —'

'Hey, Eva!' her friend Thomas called over. 'You getting them in or what?'

Brian shouted back rambunctiously. 'Hey, you!

She's talking to me, alright!' Then to Eva, just as belligerently. 'Who's your friend?'

'Thomas. A friend. You *do* know him, Brian.'

'Not as well as you do, obviously.' Brian glanced sourly down the bar. 'Never seen him before. Who the fuck is he?'

'Don't, Brian, I'm not in the mood. I don't want any more of your bad temper.'

Thomas shouted again from the other end of the bar. 'Eva! Sorry to break up your little tête-à-tête but we're dying of thirst over here.'

Eva muttered, 'I have to go, Brian.'

'Shall I come round later?'

'No, not tonight,' she replied quickly. 'I'm going out.'

'Okay, I'll phone you tomorrow then.'

'No, don't! I'll phone you.'

Brian stared after her moodily as she left his side of the bar. This was a real turnaround — Eva calling the shots.


Hans Reiner was surprised by the chaos of the kitchen when he called at the house in Monchengladbach the following morning. Used coffee-mugs on the table, a half-eaten sandwich ... All of Maureen's tidiness had been obliterated.

'So your mother is not here then?' he said to Brian.

'No, gone to Ireland.'

'Ireland?' Hans was surprised. 'Again?'

'Some more *family* business to attend to,' Brian said sarcastically.

Brian was unshaven and couldn't-care-less in his manner. 'Was it something important? Can I help?'

'Not really. I'm afraid my reason for calling was to tell her that the bank are going to call in the loan.'

'Definitely?'

'Yes, definitely.'

Brian slumped into a chair. 'Great. She buggers of to Ireland to play martyr and in the meantime we lose the house. Christ, I don't know why I even bothered to try and help her. I tell you, Hans, much more of this and I'll just bugger off and leave them to it.'

Hans regarded the young man before him with grave sternness. 'Brian, none of this is your mother's fault.'

'Yeah, right. It's easier to blame my father, isn't it?'

'No one is doing that.'

'Aren't they? I mean, hell, it wouldn't be so bad if he was here to defend himself. But he's not. And what thanks did I get for trying to help …? Someone has to take charge.'

'You mother has. In case you haven't noticed, Brian, she has been taking charge for years. She is the one who has done everything for you. Not your father.'

Brian reacted with sneering disdain. 'Don't tell me that —'

'Yes, I will tell you,' Hans replied with a quiet authority. 'Who ran the house as well as a full-time job? Who looked after you? Who sorted out your student loan? Not your father, Brian. He was never here.'

'He was running a business.'

'Yes, and your mother was helping to run a hospital.'

'It's not the same.'

'No, it's not the same. Because she was doing it successfully.'

Hans stood up to leave. 'I'm sorry, but it's about time you faced the truth. You are distressed about your father's business. You feel it was taken away from you. But believe me, it was not her fault the business had to be liquidated in the end. It was his.'

Hans opened his briefcase and took out some papers. 'Here,' he said. 'Here is the proof.'

Brian read the papers, slowly shaking his head in disbelief.

He looked up at Hans, furious. 'The scheming bastard ...'

Brian was in a foul mood when he arrived at the student bar that evening. He didn't want to go to work. What he really wanted was to punch someone

— and he saw his opportunity as soon as he had locked the door of his Volkswagen.

He saw the guy she had called Thomas — the one with the big mouth who kept shouting over to her. Now he was helping Eva and her flatmate Helen out of his car — very courteous. All three of them were laughing.

'Oi! … You!' Brian shouted.

Eva turned, sensing trouble immediately, and tried to head him off. 'Brian —'

Brian ignored her and strode up to Thomas. 'You're asking for a punch in the mouth.'

Thomas was flabbergasted. 'Says who?'

'Says me.'

Brian hit him with enough hatred in his heart to kill an army, sending him staggering back against the car.

'*Brian — stop*!' Eva grabbed him, inadvertently ripping his jacket and diverting his attention so that he didn't see Thomas launching back at him. The stunning blow Thomas cracked into his face nearly snapped his head off.

*Christ*! Brian staggered, blinked, felt a salty taste in his mouth, put a hand to his face and looked at the blood on his hand — blood that was running like a river down his nostrils.

'You sneaky fucker …' He threw himself at Thomas like a madman, grabbing him around the neck and wrestling him to the ground, both ignoring Eva and Helen's desperate cries for them to stop.

Other students ran over to see what the commotion was about, circling the two fighting men and cheering, as Eva and Helen struggled in vain to break it up, shouting for someone to help.

Finally a group of guys pulled them apart and up onto their feet, both breathing like steam engines. Both tried to lunge forward again but were held back.

'He started it!' Thomas shouted.

'So now you end it!' Eva shouted back. 'Go on, Thomas — go!'

The watching crowd began to clap; it had been a good scrap. Helen led Thomas back to the car.

Eva turned on Brian, grabbing his arm. 'You're mad! What's wrong with you?'

'Okay, okay.' He pulled himself free from her grip. 'It's over.' He turned and walked away.

She started after him. 'Is that it? Now you just walk away!'

'You want to know what's wrong with me?' He turned on her. 'You fucking want to know? Then tell me why you won't see me? Why you keep refusing to answer or return my calls? We're supposed to be in love with each other, for Christ's sake.'

'I needed some time to myself,' Eva replied with quiet seriousness. 'And it's over now, Brian. You and me … we're finished.'

Brian stood for a second looking past her; all the onlookers had drifted away. 'Do you want to tell me why?'

'I'm pregnant.'

Brian just stared at her, completely lost for words. Then, finally, 'Why didn't you tell me?'

'I *tried* to tell you!' Eva retorted angrily. 'But you were always too wrapped up with your own problems. Your dad's death, your mother's driving lessons, your sister ... angry, angry, all the time angry at everyone because of your dad's death, as if everyone was to blame for it.'

She turned to walk away; Brian followed her. 'No, no, you don't understand, I haven't told you hardly anything ... ' He caught her arm. 'Eva, at least come for a coffee somewhere and let me explain?'

A McDonald's Burger Bar was not Brian's idea of a good place to talk, but it was the nearest, and Eva had chosen it, seeming to prefer a large place with a lot of people to somewhere more intimate.

They chose a table in the far corner by the window. Eva sat stirring her polystyrene cup of coffee with its accompanying plastic stick, listening to him telling her so many things she had not known.

His father's death had been just the start of it. She was astonished to learn of the business going bankrupt, and even more shocked to hear of the impending loss of the house. And then his mother's discovery of another woman in Ireland, another child, the huge cash withdrawals every month to support them. How over the years it had bled the business dry …

Hans Reiner, the accountant, had by now also discovered that his father had bought Liza Becker her own house — with no mortgage — instead secured safely by one lump-sum cash payment. He had also bought her a new car, and just about everything else she had asked for — all paid for with money made out of the business.

'If it was all paid for in cash, how did Hans find out he bought her a new car?'

'Same way he found about the house — hidden insurance documents. All the insurance payments on the house and the car were paid directly by him. That was Dad's one big mistake. He thought he had it all covered, but he hadn't managed to hide everything.'

Brian sat back. 'So that's it. The bastard lied to us, and fooled us. All of us.'

'But the little boy …' Eva said sadly. 'You say he is sick?'


'So that explains where a lot of the money went,' Nora said to Maureen, pouring out more tea. 'The medical fees here in Ireland are dreadful. Even if you're on the medical card and your insurance pays, the cost of the tablets alone would set you back a good bit every time.'

Maureen nodded, her face thoughtful.

'And that's a private hospital the boy's in,' Nora added. 'Do you *know* how much private medi-care costs over here?'

'It doesn't matter how much it costs,' Maureen replied with a sudden burst of the old bitterness. 'She still managed to get enough out of James to pay the medical fees *and* keep herself living in comfort as well. Not to mention her designer sweaters. Jesus! The nearest I ever got to an expensive designer shop was a ride past on a bus.'

She glared at Nora. 'And you should have heard the way James used to moan about the cost of Brian's Reeboks ... or Maeve's jeans ... "Why do her jeans have to *cost* so much?" he kept asking. "Why can't she wear a skirt like other girls?"... God, when I think of it — and all the time he was paying for his fancy-woman to dress in the best.'

A heavy silence fell on the kitchen as Nora mused about it all. 'You know, it's strange,' she said finally, 'but the two don't really go together, do they?'

'Which two? James and —'

'No, no, what I mean is ...' Nora's brow was creased in perplexed thought. 'I mean, a woman sick with worry and needing every penny to pay for the medical care of her sick little boy, yet still goes out and buys herself expensive clothes ... The two don't go together, do they?'

'No,' Maureen had to agree. 'No they don't, come to think of it.'

'But then,' Nora added slowly. 'Out in her own community in Bray, she's been living a lie all these years. And like most people who lie, she obviously wanted to cover it well.'

Maureen could do nothing else but stare at Nora, who continued, 'Now *you* know, more than anyone else does, Maureen, that it's not in my nature to speak ill of anyone.'

Maureen nodded. It was definitely not in Nora's nature

'And I'm still not speaking ill of anyone either,' Nora insisted. 'All I'm saying is what I think. And I think this Liza Becker has been living for some time with a very guilty conscience she desperately wants to hide — probably even from herself.'

Bray, windy from the sea-breeze and dark with night. All but the promenade was bright with lights, the hotels and guest houses which lined the seafront full with tourists.

Liza was enjoying the drive out to Bray, the speed of the car, the break from the hospital. She arrived at the church hall of St Mary's School just as the choir was finishing practice for the night.

Slipping inside the hall, she saw Michael folding up the conductor's music stand, and placing it near the stacked chairs, while other members of the choir collected up empty coffee mugs. The conductor was amusing himself, improvising at the piano. The sound of his happy tinkling cheered her as she made her way over to Michael.

'Michael?'

He looked round. 'Well, this is a pleasant surprise. But what about —'

'Jamie's sleeping,' she said. 'I just thought I'd slip out for a bit. Take a break, you know.'

'Yeah, sure.' Michael was glad she had done so.

A young man, Paddy O'Sheehan, who had a voice like a tenor's dream, tapped Liza on the shoulder.

'So how is the little fella, Liza? I hear you may have a donor?'

'Yes, he's great, Paddy.' She smiled at Michael. 'It looks like the transplant is going to take place tomorrow.'

'Really? Oh well then, this calls for a celebration drink,' Michael exclaimed. 'Come on. You too, Paddy.'

Paddy looked dubious. 'But you don't drink, Michael.'

'I do. Orange juice. And tonight I'm going to celebrate with a double!'

Paddy looked even more dubious. 'And you, Liza, in the pub, what are you going to drink?'

'What I normally drink,' Liza smiled. 'A double Powers whiskey.'

'That's my girl,' Paddy grinned, clapping his hands. 'That's the way to celebrate. Michael — lead the way.'

In Düsseldorf, the staff at McDonalds had started to wipe down the tables and mop the floor in readiness to close, and only a few people remained chatting at tables.

Eva was observing Brian's face with a strange wonder. Throughout their conversation and almost before her eyes, she had watched the right side of his face change colour to a dark purplish hue, and now the swollen lid of his right eye was closing down fast.

'You look terrible,' she said.

Brian shrugged; he didn't care.

'You don't have to worry,' she said quietly. 'I'll be having an abortion.'

'No, no, don't, please. No.' He shook his head desperately. 'I don't want you to have an abortion. I want you to keep the baby.'

'Don't be stupid. What are we going to live on?'

'I'll get a job. A proper job, not part-time behind a bar. Just tell me — do you still love me?'

'Yes,' she replied, simply.

'And do you want to keep the baby?'

'Yes.'

'Then keep it, because, believe me, Eva, I'll be there for you, every step of the way. I promise.'

'Like you've been there for your mother?' Eva's

small smile was caustic. 'Accusing her, every step of the way. Not caring how much she hurt. Feeling only your own hurt. Even now. It's all about you, isn't it, Brian?'

Brian lapsed into a silence, knowing everything she said was the truth.

'You can't be here for me, Brian, or this baby. You can't do anything for anyone, not even for yourself. Not until you realise that it's about time you stopped being your father's son and grew up.'

She moved to her feet, turned and walked out. Brian made no attempt to follow her.

Maeve, Jenny and Niamh were still full of high spirits when they got home from Temple Bar.

Sean was fed up with them and their girlish noise. 'Like squealing cats, yous were, the three of you, all the way home,' he complained. 'No one ever told me these Cranberries were worth squealing about.'

'Da, they're just *brilliant*!' Niamh exclaimed. 'Why do you have to be so old-fashioned?'

He gave her an affronted look. 'Who's old-fashioned? Not me, Niamh. I'm the man who started it all rolling.'

Maeve was still giggling when she ran up the stairs and breezed into the bedroom — stopping dead at the sight of her mother packing a suitcase.

Maureen looked round and checked her watch.

'Well, this is a first. Home on time! What happened?'

'Sean was outside waiting for us, sending in messages to us, we had to leave before the end. Mum, why are you packing that suitcase?'

'It's for you. For the hospital tomorrow. They may want you to stay over.'

Maeve laughed and began pulling off her clothes. 'Mum, they just put a needle in your back. It's not open heart surgery. There's enough stuff in that case for a month.'

'Still, better safe than sorry.'

Maureen stood watching her daughter as she changed into her night clothes. 'So, are you nervous, Maeve?'

Maeve sat down on the bed, suddenly serious. 'Yeah, I am a bit. But I'm excited too. I like what I'm doing.'

'And what you're doing … it's a good thing, Maeve.'

Maureen turned her eyes back to the suitcase, struggling inside herself to find the right words. 'I've been thinking … about the boy, Jamie. I know how much you want to meet him, Maeve. So I'll talk to Michael Docherty and see if he can arrange it.'

A smile of pure delight spread across Maeve's astonished face. She jumped off the bed and grabbed her mother into a tight hug. 'Oh, Mum!'

Brian was still sitting in McDonald's, showing no reaction to the dirty looks of the staff as they cleaned around him. He wasn't even aware of them. He was gazing at the plate glass of the dark window, seeing the reflection of a young man, who happened to be himself.

He'd got it all wrong. He hadn't got the world taped after all. It was in an even bigger fucking mess than he had originally thought.

He sat gazing numbly at his reflection. The death of his father was nothing to this; nothing to the loss of Eva. Suddenly he forgot his own misery in a rush of sorrow for Eva. What these past few weeks must have been like for her, finding out she was pregnant and not knowing what to do. Keep it? Or abort it? Who to turn to? Not her selfish *schlemiel* of a boyfriend, that was for sure.

He continued staring at his reflection, searching for some kind of excuse for himself and his behaviour.

Then suddenly, in an image his mind brought back from the past, he saw the face of a proud young boy who had idolised his father, like a god upon high, certain that the future was held safely in his own two strong and trustworthy hands. His first and only hero … Well, that was one childish myth he intended to abandon.

Finally he stood up and left McDonald's, his mind rushing with thoughts as he drove back home.

Once there, he went straight up to his mother's

bedroom, opened the bottom of the spare wardrobe and pulled out the two black refuse sacks filled with his father's clothes — the clothes he had prevented his mother from giving to Oxfam …. *Christ, Mum, show him some respect!*

Swept on by a revulsion of feeling against himself and his father, he dragged the bags down the stairs and out into the back garden, dumping them on the grass before rummaging in the shed, coming back out a few moments later carrying a large bottle of barbecue lighter fuel.

He pushed the bags down into the metal refuse bin and sprinkled them liberally with the fuel — not in anger, but clearly and calmly enough to have the sense to carry the bottle of fuel back to the safety of the shed.

Then he returned, took a box of matches from his pocket and lit one, dropping it onto the pile of clothes. A small blue flame appeared, then an eruption of fire only inches away from his face. He stepped back, watching his father's clothes go up in smoke.


Feeling good, relaxed by her double shot of whiskey, Liza crept into the oncology ward, past the other curtained-off beds, and slipped inside the curtains where Jamie was fast asleep in his bed.

Smiling, she stared down on the Gameboy still in his hand; still 'chirping' away. He must have fallen asleep during a game. She switched it off and lifted it away.

'Mrs Becker.'

She turned.

Dr Brady was standing behind her, holding back the curtain.

'Oh, Dr Brady,' she said with surprise. 'My God, you're working late aren't —'

Her voice dried to a croak. Even before Dr Brady spoke, she knew what he had come to say.

'I'm sorry, Mrs Becker. The final results have just come in. I'm afraid it's bad news …'

No, no — she wanted to turn away and cover her ears but all she could do was stare at him, ashen-faced, in dread.

'The girl. She isn't a good-enough match. So I'm sorry to say there will be no transplant for Jamie tomorrow. It's just not close enough to risk it. I'm sorry.'

# TWENTY-TWO

Early the next morning, after leaving the hospital, Michael Docherty conveyed the news personally to Maeve and Maureen.

'No transplant?' Maeve looked devastated.

'It's not Jamie's body that's rejecting your marrow,' Michael explained, 'but the white cells in your marrow, in your immune defence system, not recognising Jamie's body and attacking it.'

Michael paused. 'I've not explained that very well, have I? I'm trying to remember and repeat what Dr Brady said. But, essentially, what it means is that the transplant would reject ... It's no one's fault, Maeve, honestly.'

Maeve nodded, clearly upset. 'But Jamie knows I tried to help him, doesn't he? Jamie knows who I am?'

Michael and Maureen exchanged a swift glance at each other, then Michael lied, 'Of course Jamie knows who you are, Maeve.'

Maureen reached out to take Maeve's hand and comfort her. 'But what about Brian?' Maeve said. 'Brian could still be a match, couldn't he?'

The question hung in the air. Maureen tried to

221

speak but no words came out. Maeve looked at Michael. 'Brian could, couldn't he? Tell her.'

Michael knew that what Maeve said was the truth, and for a moment he had difficulty endeavouring to quell his own renewed hope. But he also knew that the brother would be a far harder nut to crack than the girl, having already refused to have anything to do with it.

Apart from that, Michael had no real willingness to upset Maureen Lessing further, not in any way. She had her axe to grind, understandably so, but she had come through with the girl in the end. She had done her best. Could they now ask for more?

Maeve obviously thought so, tugging at her mother's arm with a desperate plea. 'Tell her, Mr Docherty, tell her that Jamie could have another chance with Brian.'

'Well, another chance, possibly. But that's not to say —'

'You see!' Maeve swung to Maureen. 'Mum — you'll just have to *make* Brian come to Ireland and do it!'

Maureen was confused and unsure of what to say or do. Michael Docherty came to her rescue and said it for her.

'Maeve, at fifteen, you are not legally an adult, that's why you could not have agreed to do this without your mother's permission. But your brother *is* an adult. Your mother can't force him to do anything, no matter what she or you or I think.

Besides, we don't know for sure that he'd even be a match.'

'What will you do now?' Maureen asked.

Michael shrugged. 'Well, we'll never stop hoping. And we haven't given up looking.'

An awkward silence fell on the room; there was really nothing more to say. Michael stood up. 'I'd better get back.'

'I'll see you out,' Maureen said.

Maureen walked with him to the door of his car. 'It was good of you to come personally, Mr Docherty. I appreciate it.'

He gave her a small smile. 'Could you not call me Michael?'

'What you said to Maeve in there, about the boy knowing …?'

'Don't worry. He doesn't.'

'And about Brian. I'll phone and ask him. It's all I can do … ask.'

Michael was completely taken aback, his hope rising again. 'Oh, thank you. Thank you.'

Maureen smiled slightly, a flush colouring her cheeks, embarrassed by the joy on his face. She turned abruptly and walked back inside.

Back in Monchengladbach, Brian was just leaving the house, double-locking the door behind him as usual.

Less than five minutes after he had left, the

223

telephone in the house started to ring … and continued to ring incessantly every fifteen minutes for three hours.

Maureen replaced her mobile phone on the bedside cabinet and stood up to talk to Maeve who was painting her toenails in the bathroom.

'He's still not there. I'll try again later.'

'You promise.'

'But if he says no, Maeve, we have to accept it and go home, okay?'

'I don't see why we can't just stay here.'

'Stay here?' Maureen laughed at the absurdity of the suggestion.

'It's not that funny,' Maeve insisted. 'I mean, there's sod all but bills left for us in Germany.'

'What about your friends at school?'

'Mum, we both know I'm not going to be able to stay there. How could we afford the fees?'

Maureen was surprised by Maeve's sudden maturity; as if the failed transplant had changed her.'

'Besides, give me Dublin any day,' Maeve continued. 'At least they've got some decent bands and clubs and Jenny reckons I could go to her school, no problem.'

'Maybe so, but it's not just about you, Maeve. I have my job and my own friends in Germany to consider. I'm not ready to just drop my work and my friends in the same way I had to do in England ten years ago, because your father decided to move to Düsseldorf .'

Maeve shot a contrite look at her mother, realising how selfish her suggestion must have sounded.

She shrugged it off with a grin. 'Just a joke, Mum.'


In the paediatric oncology ward, Liza searched through the lunch trolley for the tray with Jamie's name on it ...

Jamie stood grumpily beside her, attached to a platelet pump. 'So I won't be having my transplanting today?'

'Not for a little bit, no.'

'Or my new bike?'

'Oh yes, you'll still get your bike.'

'Great!' The announcement of this good news cheered Jamie up immediately. He shouted to the nurse. 'I still get my new bike!'

Liza lifted out his tray and looked at the contents. 'It's pizza.'

'Yeah! *Pizza*! My *favourite*!' Jamie's joy was flowing now. 'It's my lucky day!'

Lucky day? ... Liza turned her head away, not wanting Jamie to see her sudden tears.

# TWENTY-THREE

Bridget had just finished her hoovering of the stairs when Nora answered the front doorbell to a young couple.

'I'm sorry,' Nora apologised. 'We're completely booked.'

'Could you recommend anywhere else?' asked the man.

'The Town House,' Nora smiled. She stepped out and indicated. 'About a hundred yards down, on the other side. It's very nice.'

'Right. Thank you. Bye now.'

Nora turned back into the hall to face Bridget's disapproving stare. 'So are they going back to Germany today or what?'

'We don't know yet,' Nora replied, setting off down the hall to the dining room.

Bridget followed her into the dining room, complaining, 'Because at the moment we should be on commission for the bloody Town House, the amount of people we're sending there.'

Sean looked round from fixing a light socket in the wall, immediately sensing trouble. His mother had been told nothing about what was really going on, and now she was showing signs of her ignorance.

'I mean,' Bridget continued, 'this morning they're going and now they're not. Has everyone forgotten that we're trying to run a hotel here? A business, like.'

Sean looked at Nora — his mother deserved to be told.

'Bridget, the sick little boy in hospital,' Nora said. 'He's connected to the family.'

'What?' Bridget stared at Nora, totally mystified. 'He's connected to the family? How can that be?'

Nora lost her nerve and abdicated. 'Sean will explain it all to you.'

'Me?' Sean stared at his wife in utter surprise.

Nora nodded. 'Go on, Sean, tell your mother.'

Seeing no way out of it, Sean took up the responsibility by taking his mother by the hand and sitting her down.

'Now, I want you to listen, Ma, very carefully, because this is important ...' He then tried to explain about James Lessing and Liza Becker.

'What? You mean — Maureen's husband was an adulterer?'

'You've got to forget all that and look at this from the boy's side. Whether we like it or not, James Lessing had another family in Bray. And the wee boy who's so sick, is his son. That's why Maeve was ready to give him the transplant. The sick boy is her half-brother.'

'My God ... and how long has Maureen known all this?'

'Only since she first came here, after James Lessing's death.'

'Ah, God ...' the tears began to well up in Bridget's eyes as she finally realised. 'No wonder poor Maureen couldn't eat anything.'

Back in the ward, Liza and Jamie were going through the daily routine of his mouth swabs.

Liza lifted the pink squirt-bottle.

Jamie shut his mouth tight, pulling a face.

'Come on, Jamie.'

Jamie shook his head.

Liza tried to make a game of it, advancing on him with the bottle. 'Open wide. Come on, if you want your new bike, a deal is a deal ...'

Jamie opened his mouth.

Liza squirted the medication in.

'There now, all done.'

A moment later Jamie gagged, and threw the whole lot back up over her.

Maureen put down the phone and walked back into the kitchen, shaking her head at Nora and Sean.

'Brian's still not there.'

'Ah, he'll be back soon I'm sure,' Bridget opined. She was happier now that she knew the truth. She cut into a freshly baked cake, laid a thick slice on a plate, and handed it to Maureen. 'Probably out somewhere with his girlfriend.'

Sean smiled questioningly at his mother. 'Any chance of a slice of that cake for me? For the head of the house, like?' He glanced round at Nora. 'And pop the kettle on there, will you, Nora, like a good girl.'

Nora gave him an indignant look. 'Why don't you "pop" it on yourself, or are you paralysed from the waist down?'

'From the neck up, more like,' Bridget muttered.

The front door buzzer prevented Sean's reply. He stood up, not offended, smiling at Maureen. 'Family love, isn't it a grand thing.'

A flash of concern on his face as he realised what he had just said. Maureen laughed it off.

'They love you really, Sean.'

Sean diverted his eyes to Nora. 'The front door — I'll go then, will I? I mean, I wouldn't like to overtire you or anything. That wouldn't be fair, especially as you don't have to slave at a second job as a cab driver, like myself. No, Nora, you just relax, rest your legs, I'll see to the door.'

His sarcasm was completely ignored.

'If it's that Inspector Clouseau and he's lost his key again, leave him out there. Teach him a lesson,' Bridget called after him.

Bridget winked at Maureen and immediately sat

down beside her. 'Now then ... Sean and Nora have told me all about your troubles.'

Maureen flushed guiltily. 'Bridget, I'm sorry, I should have told you but I didn't want —'

'No! Not a word.' Bridget held up her hand to stop any further explanations. 'I just want you to know that I'm sorry, Maureen, sorry for you and your troubles, and you are welcome to stay here for as long as you like.'

Maureen nodded, touched by her generosity. 'Thanks, Bridget.'

'Now,' Bridget coaxed, 'how about eating some of this cake?'

Sean was detained at the bottom of the hall stairs by a couple of English guests.

'Excuse me,' said the husband. 'You don't do evening meals, do you?'

'Correct. We don't.' Sean smiled apologetically.

'It's just the breakfasts here are so good, we thought perhaps —'

The front door buzzer became insistent. 'No, I'm sorry,' Sean said quickly. 'Excuse me.'

He opened the front door.

'Hello, Sean.'

A young man whom he did not recognise stood before him, with a bruised face and swollen right eye. 'Sorry, we're fully booked,' he said.

The young man grinned. 'Sean, it's me, Brian Lessing. Don't you remember? Maureen's son.'

'In the name of —!' Sean exclaimed, delighted. 'Come in, come in, Brian. We've all been thinking about you.'

'Maureen! *Maureen*!' Sean called out excitedly. 'Maeve! Your brother is here … Maeve …?'

Brian dropped his rucksack in the hall and turned to get his bearings. He had not been in this house since he was a child, and everything looked completely different.

'Brian …' Maureen rushed into the hall, her face full of disbelief. 'Brian, what are you doing here? God, what happened to your face?'

Brian gave his sheepish grin. 'A slight accident. Looks like I gave Sean a bit of a shock too.'

'Jesus, you did,' Sean said. 'You were the *last* person I expected to see at the door, especially as she's been trying to phone you about —'

'Brian,' Maureen interrupted. 'There's something I urgently need to discuss with you.'

Brian agreed.

Maureen was so surprised she didn't really believe him. There had been no protestations, no anger, just a simple agreement to do what was right.

'Only I don't want to make a big deal of it,' Brian said. 'I don't want you to tell the kid or his mother that the donor is me. Okay?'

231

'Okay.' Maureen was beaming. She hugged him to her, full of love.

Maeve walked in a second later and — much to Brian's chagrin — clenched her raised fists and let out a scream of delight.

'*Yes*!'


The hospital went into action immediately.

Dr Brady's eyes carefully watched the vacuum pump syringe filling up with Brian's blood, then withdrew the needle, capped the vacuum pump, and handed it to a nurse for labelling.

'A few hours and we should know,' he said to Brian and Maureen; then he took the bottle from the nurse and swiftly disappeared — on his way to the haematology laboratory where he later stood and watched a centrifuge full of phials of Brian's blood spinning faster and faster …

Brian and Maureen went to get a cup of tea while they waited for the results.

'I wonder how they do it,' Brian murmured curiously; unaware that at that moment his 'bloods' were being passed through the magnetic bars of the complex computer machinery that separates off the marrow T-cells.

Maureen was very tense, and her face showed it.

Brian pulled the plaster off his arm and sat looking around at the people waiting to be called for the various clinics.

Suddenly he caught sight of a man walking into the Tea Bar and heading directly for their table. Thinking he must be some kind of doctor, Brian murmured, 'Here we go. I think the results are in.'

Maureen turned her head, and saw Michael Docherty.

Michael's gratitude was undisciplined. He shook Brian's hand strongly. 'Brian, nice to meet you. I want to thank you for your help.'

Brian shot a look at his mother — no one was supposed to know.

Michael Docherty quickly reassured him. 'It's all right, Liza doesn't know you are here. So I suppose my thanks are on her behalf as well.'

Brian nodded, but did not speak.

Michael saw instantly that Brian was still wary of him, still a hard nut to crack.

Maureen attempted to cover the awkward silence. 'We're just waiting for the results,' she said.

In the Mullen's house, Maeve was endeavouring to earn her keep, hoovering the carpets.

She switched off the hoover when she saw Nora coming down the hall carrying a pile of clean towels for the bedrooms.

'Any news?' Maeve asked anxiously.

'Not yet. But don't worry, you'll know as soon as there is. Bridget is on guard by the phone.'

To eat away the time, Maureen and Brian took a stroll around the hospital grounds.

Maureen murmured, 'You know that you have made Maeve very happy.'

Brian's grin was sardonic. 'That's a first then.'

'She does love you, you know. Despite what she says.'

Brian shrugged, looking away. During these past few hours of waiting for the results, his mother and himself seemed to have drawn closer, and he was glad of it. He thought that maybe now was the time to walk their own slow way round to a real reconciliation.

'I should apologise to you,' he said with quiet graveness. 'Eva accused me of patronising you, treating you like a fool, and taking over. And she was right. Now I think I understand why I did it. I tried to take over and establish my authority because I resented being excluded all the time. The private financial details you could only discuss with Hans Reiner. You flying off to Ireland with Maeve. Too busy to answer my phone calls. While I was left in Germany looking around for smart answers and ending up clueless. I was angry and I resented it, childishly so, in the circumstances.'

Maureen's heart was beating fast. 'I tried to keep it all from you because I knew how much you loved and respected your father. I didn't want to poison that.'

'All my anger about Dad's death was directed

against you,' Brian continued. 'I even found myself blaming you for his infidelity. That was unfair. Only Dad can be held responsible for that. But all the other stuff — the moods, the temper — I'm sorry, Mum.'

Maureen had tears in her eyes. 'Brian, I can't tell you … I feel such a weight has been lifted.'

Brian looked around for something to focus his eyes upon, wondering if he should now tell her about Eva being pregnant and his own decision to leave college and home and apply for a full-time job at Ericcsons. They would give him time off to complete his computer studies, one day a week, he was sure of that.

'From the day you were born I've always loved you,' Maureen said. 'I want you to know that, Brian. I love you. And apart from these last weeks, you've always been a good son.'

Brian shook his head, disclaiming the compliment. 'Most of the time I've been a prize prick. But now I want to talk to you seriously, about what I've decided to do with my life …'

They talked earnestly and intimately together — of plans and possibilities — until Brian's attention was distracted by the sight of a man walking with a hurried step towards them down the path. He wore a white hospital coat with the leads of a stethoscope trailing from one of its pockets. Definitely a doctor this time.

A few steps closer and Brian recognised him as

the man who had done the blood tests. Dr Brady. His hand was raised.

'Mr Lessing!' he called out. 'It's good news!'

Only then, after speaking with Brian, did Dr Brady, accompanied by Michael Docherty, take the news to Liza.

She stared uncomprehendingly at the two smiling men standing at the end of Jamie's bed.

'Good news ... What good news?'

'We've found a donor, Mrs Becker. It's not perfect, but I think we have to go with it ...'

'A donor? I don't understand ... How? Where ...?'

Michael was simply beaming. 'Who cares. We've got a good donor, that's all that counts. And this time, Liza — it's going to work.'

# TWENTY-FOUR

In the X-Ray room, Brian stood sandwiched between the magnetic plates.

'Hold very still now,' the radiologist commanded. 'Very still.'

*Click.*

'Perfect.'


'Don't move ... Stay still, Jamie,' Liza commanded through a microphone.

Inside the TBI chamber, Jamie lay very still on the radiologist's table, his body marked with felt-tip blue crosses, his head shielded by lead blocks.

'Mammy ... I'm frightened ... Mammy.'

Distressed, Liza watched through the TV monitor, gripping one of the radiologist's hands for support as she spoke into the microphone again, her voice strong and encouraging.

'Not long now, Jamie ... Good boy, don't move ...'


Jamie was moved into the Transplant Prep Unit an hour later. It was a three-bed unit, plus a tiny kitchen and a nurses' room. Beyond it were two sets of double doors leading to the Isolation Unit and its cubicles.

Jamie had fallen asleep in his new bed.

Liza stood with Michael Docherty by the second set of double doors, looking through to the isolation cubicles.

'How long now?' Michael asked.

'Hopefully, later this afternoon.'

'That's great.'

'Yes.' Liza turned back towards the Prep Unit. 'I still can't believe it. It's happened so fast. I thought the likelihood of finding another donor was slight.'

'But not impossible, thank God.'

Liza looked at him. 'I thought you didn't believe in God.'

Michael smiled. 'To be honest, I'm too buzzed up to know what I believe anymore.'

'It's *you* I should thank,' Liza said. 'For everything you've done.'

'Hey, forget it. What are friends for?'

She quickly turned and hugged him. 'You're a good man, Michael. That's rare these days.'

'You may think that now, but give it time, Liza. There's plenty of good men around. You just have to look in the right places.'

For the briefest of moments, the depth of his feelings for her came into his eyes.

She smiled, and pulled gently away from him. His eyes had told her nothing that she didn't already know.

Along another corridor, Brian was being wheeled on a trolley towards the operating theatre. Maureen and Maeve walked each side of him, amused by his embarrassment.

'I could have walked,' he insisted.

'What!' exclaimed the porter good-humouredly. 'And do me out of a job. Get away with you. If all the patients talked like you I'd be made redundant, so I would.'

The trolley came to a halt. The porter opened the double doors that bore a large sign: *No Admittance*.

'Well, this is it,' Brian said.

Impulsively, Maeve bent down, hugging and kissing him.

Brian pushed her off with a grin. 'Well that's a good enough reason for not doing this every day.'

Maeve gave a laugh. 'Up yours.'

Maureen squeezed his hand. 'See you in a bit, Brian. You'll be fine.'

The porter wheeled him in.

A short time later, Brian lay out motionless on the operating table while Mr Brady slowly extracted a hollow needle from the back of his hip-bone and examined it. 'That should be plenty.'

He turned and handed it to the Sister. 'Get that down to Haematology for cleaning, please, Sister. And then let's just hope we get lucky.'

In the Düsseldorf bank, Hans Reiner doggedly kept

stride beside the bank manager, who clearly had no time for him as he hurried towards the lift on his way to a meeting, busily exchanging papers with his assistant.

'Mr Reiner, I really don't see the point in going over it all again. Nothing has changed.'

'Mrs Lessing has suggested using the insurance money she gets for the car in part-settlement of her debt.'

The manager handed another paper to his assistant. 'And can you make sure this is faxed to head office.' He glanced irritably at Hans. 'The car insurance? Unfortunately that would hardly pay off her mortgage arrears let alone the interest on her loan.'

'Bankrupting her won't help. She is trying to reduce her expenditure. But with two children ...'

Hans followed the manager into the lift, obliging him to listen further.

'Mr Reiner, we have tried to be sympathetic but we have nothing to gain by giving her more time.'

'Sympathetic?' Hans exclaimed angrily. 'I don't call digging around in her rubbish bin and worrying her half to death *sympathetic*.'

The manager looked at Hans Reiner's face, scrutinising it shrewdly, a small sardonic smile appearing on his lips.

'I must say, Mr Reiner, for an accountant you seem to be taking this very personally.'

'Yes, well ...'

The lift stopped. The manager quickly stepped out and, in swift succession, bid Hans a curt goodbye and pressed the button for the lift doors to close and go back down.

Well it *is* personal, Hans thought, as he descended to the ground floor. He had always liked Maureen and since James Lessing's death they had grown much closer. And he had always surmised that Maureen liked him too ...

Hans sucked in his bottom lip, thinking of the coy way she had thanked him for the flowers, her cheeks blushing ... By the time he stepped out of the lift, he had reached a decision.

Yes, he *would* ask Maureen. Oh, not to marry him, too soon for that. But to *depend* on him. After all, they were both getting on in years. Companionship and sexual partners were not that easy to come by at fifty plus.

Yes ... He nodded his head in confirmation. That's what he would do. He would ask her to *depend* upon him. And although she would obviously not agree to a marriage, she may well agree to a honeymoon. Now where, he wondered, was a good place to go on a fishing honeymoon in September or October? Possibly even November? Scotland was very good for salmon. Or maybe he could even stretch himself to a honeymoon in Canada ... wonderful fishing in northern Canada. A place she had never been or seen — she would love it! She'd be so happy she might even enjoy the fishing.

Hans stopped walking. But first ... he needed some fishing tackle and bait to catch his lovely plump trout ... and that bait, he suddenly realised, was Maureen's house. Hans turned around and retraced his steps to the bank.

The manager's assistant regarded him warily. 'I'm afraid the manager is —'

'Don't worry,' Hans said cheerfully. 'I'll wait.'

It was almost six o'clock when Sean Mullen checked his watch and speeded his steps along the hospital corridor, carrying an enormous bag of fruit.

He stopped a young nurse. 'Excuse me, Sister, would you happen to know where Brian Lessing might be?'

'Is he a patient?'

'No, he's a donor. Somewhere in the bone marrow transplanting section. He's just had an operation. Would you happen to know what ward he's in?'

The nurse looked at him sideways, a smile in her eyes. 'I think it might be quicker all round if I just took you straight there, don't you?'

'That'd be grand. Thanks, Sister.'

She took him to a small unit used for patients recovering from minor operations.

Sean hurried in, and stopped — surprised to Brian already up and dressed, talking to Maureen and Maeve.

'You're up?'

Brian nodded. 'Have been for an hour. Nothing to it.'

Sean could barely conceal his disappointment … He had expected tension, fear, a life-or-death drama. That was why, just an hour earlier, he had nipped into the café where most of the cabbies took their break and told them all about it. About how his young cousin was — '*at this very moment*' —lying in an operating theatre giving up a piece of his bone-marrow so's it could be transplanted into a sick little boy … And all the cabbies had thought it a great thing for Sean's relative to do. And brave, they all had agreed. '*Very brave.*'

But now it looked as if the whole thing was no big deal at all. Sean stared suspiciously at Brian. 'Are you sure you're not feeling pain or anything?'

'No, just a bit stiff.' Brian grinned. 'Like I said, nothing to it.'

The nurse spoke in a low voice to Maureen, her eye on Brian. 'You wait till tonight. He won't be so chirpy then. Not when the pain and stiffness really kicks in.'

By the time he was allowed to leave the hospital an hour later, Brian could already feel the stiffness down his right side. He walked gingerly to Sean's Espace taxi at a slow pace.

Now *this* was more like it. Sean brightened, and called out cheerfully. 'Are you all right there, Brian?'

'Fine, Sean.'

'Let me take your arm,' Maureen insisted.

Brian gently moved her hand away. 'Mum, there's absolutely no need. I'm just feeling a bit stiff, that's all.'

'No pain?'

'None whatsoever.'

Jamie had been moved into his own isolation cubicle. A small room filled with the constant humming sound of a Positive Airflow pump.

Jamie sat up in bed, excited as he channel-hopped the TV which was suspended outside the glass wall of the room.

'Look, Mam, I got my own remote control!'

How easily the young are amused, Liza thought. How little it took to distract them from all worry, all danger.

'Your own remote control! Isn't that great!' Liza smiled at her son. She was now gowned in her sterile tracksuit, overslippers and cap.

Her eyes moved over the spotlessly clean surfaces of the sterile room, and realised she would have little work to do here. Not a germ could survive in it.

'Look, Mum, *Rugrats*! I've got my own cartoon channel!'

'Don't get so excited,' Liza urged, but he was lost in the television, ignoring her.

She turned to look out at the setting sun and saw the night shadows approaching. Would she sleep tonight? How could she? Tomorrow was the day she had been praying for … Transplant day.

Down below in the hospital grounds, her eyes were suddenly drawn to a small group of people getting into a car … Maureen Lessing, helping a young man into the front seat.

Liza was startled. She was sure Michael had told her that Maureen Lessing and Maeve had gone back to Germany … The young man turned, as if insisting that he didn't need any help, and that's when Liza saw his face clearly, and instantly knew who he was.

The similarity was striking. Not only to James, but also to Jamie … An older version of Jamie. His donor too … No wonder the match was so good.

The realisation filled Liza with a wild joy and an abundance of hope, a swelling of pure gratitude.

And yet, as she looked down at Brian Lessing getting into the car unassisted, Liza felt a stab of guilt as she remembered all the times she had vehemently wished that he and his sister did not exist.

# TWENTY-FIVE

Sean stopped his glass halfway to his lips.

'*A certain person,*' he declared solemnly, 'has been making very unfunny wisecracks about me all night. And if she doesn't put a sock in it forthwith, I'll be forced to send her on a very long *vayyy-cation* to an old folk's retirement home!'

'Forthwith!' Bridget laughed hilariously. 'Wasn't I right to send to him to the Jesuits for his education. *Forthwith*! Oh, Father Francis would be so proud if he could hear him now.'

Everyone was laughing. They had all enjoyed a delectable supper. And now there were two empty bottles of sparkling wine on the table and Nora was opening another.

'Jenny, don't drain your glass with your head back like that,' Nora reprimanded. 'It's unmannerly.'

'No, it's not — it's empty!' Jenny laughed, holding up her glass for some more.

Only Brian stood separate from the merriment of the celebration, speaking quietly into the telephone in the corner, a hand over his ear to block out the conversation in the room.

Maureen poured some wine into a glass and

246

carried it over to him, placing the glass on the window-ledge beside him.

'He's looking pale,' Bridget remarked, then called over, 'You need something with a bit more bite in it, young fella, not that fizzy rubbish.' She got up and opened a cupboard, taking out a bottle of Irish whiskey.

'Bridget!' Nora put a hand out to prevent Bridget from opening the bottle, but Sean was in full agreement with his mother.

'It'll do him the world of good. Help him to relax. And anyway, it's a celebration.'

Bridget leaned over to Maureen and whispered, 'Who's Brian talking to?'

Maureen smiled; she had heard Brian say Eva's name a couple of times, so concluded, 'He's talking to his girlfriend, Bridget.'

'His *girl*friend! Oh huroosh, hurray, and who better?' Bridget carried a large whiskey over to Brian and handed it to him. 'There you go, lad, get that down you.'

'Oh, thanks ...' Brian looked as if he would prefer to refuse, but Bridget used his moment of distraction to grab the receiver out of his hand.

'Listen, my girl,' she said into the phone. 'Your young man is a hero. Deserves a medal, so he does. And I tell you, if I was twenty years younger, I'd marry him myself. God bless you!'

Winking wickedly, she handed the receiver back to an embarrassed Brian, who turned away for privacy. 'Eva, sorry, she just grabbed the phone. Eva … are you there …?'

'*Twenty years* younger?' Sean levelled a pitiful smile at his mother. 'Sure even if you were that much younger, you'd *still* be twenty years too old for him.'

'Ah, get knotted you,' Bridget laughed.


In Jamie's isolation room, the lights of Dublin city were visible from the window. Liza turned away from the night sights and moved back to Jamie's bed and stood watching him devoutly holding his remote control in both hands as he stared at the television hung outside his room, the remains of his supper tray beside him.

'Have you finished with this?'

He nodded. 'Can I have a video now?'

'Yes. A cartoon video. After your drink. What do you want?'

'*Rugrats.*'

'To drink!'

No response.

Liza smiled to herself as she began to clear up the tray — suddenly stopping and freezing all her movements as she saw Dr Brady walk into the ante-room outside.

She stared at him, her heart quivering in her throat … Oh no, this could not be happening again!

Dr Brady turned away from the nurse, and

looked directly at Liza, smiling. He held up an innocuous-looking clear plastic bag of pale blood against the window.

The marrow transplant had arrived.


Nora was making coffee and teas, while Bridget ignored Maureen's protest and tried to pour some whiskey into her glass.

'No. No. Honestly. Give it to Sean.'

'What, and waste good whiskey?' Bridget poured some into her own glass.

Sean looked dryly at Maeve and his two laughing daughters. 'Oh, yeah, yous can laugh now. But I'm the one who'll be suffering with her hangover in the morning.'

'So, it will make a pleasant change from suffering with your own, won't it,' Bridget retorted. She stood up. 'I'm away to me bed.'

Brian stood also. 'I think I'll go up too.'

Maureen looked at him, concerned. 'Are you okay, Brian? You've been very quiet all night.'

Brian was utterly depressed, because Eva was still insisting upon having the abortion. And on top of that, he could now feel the pain seeping into his hip.

'I'm fine,' he said. 'Just a bit tired, that's all.'

'He can walk me up to my room,' Bridget said, then winked at Jenny and Niamh. 'I might even invite him in if he plays his cards right.'

'Bridget!' Nora gasped.

But the two girls loved it, emitting a series of wolf whistles and cheers which followed Bridget and Brian all the way up the stairs.

Maureen put her elbows on the table and covered her blushing face with her hands. 'Poor Brian, he'll be *so* embarrassed.'

'So, tell us,' Jenny said eagerly. 'What's his girlfriend like?'

'Gorgeous!' Maeve replied boastfully. 'She's blonde and German and *really* cool.'

In the isolation room, only the dimmed angled lamp near the bed illuminated Liza as she sat watching over the sleeping Jamie, her eyes fixed on the life-saving bone marrow slowly infusing down the Hickman line and into his chest.

Occasionally she stroked his brow, thinking he was like a sick little bird who needed a lot of love and care to make him better.

And occasionally she thought of the young man and girl who had done so much to try and help him.

Sean was stacking the dishwasher while Nora and Maureen laid the table in preparation for the morning's rushed family breakfast before the serving of the tourists in the dining-room began. The three girls had gone upstairs for a last chat before sleeping.

'Sorry about Bridget,' Nora said. 'She can get a bit lively with a drink in her.'

Maureen laughed. 'No, don't apologise. I love it. Reminds me of home.'

Sean glanced over his shoulder. 'You should have seen her last Christmas. Got stuck into the sherry bottle and forgot to put the turkey in the oven. Jesus, that was a classic.'

'You're lucky to have such a wonderful family.'

'Yeah,' Sean agreed. 'It's mad here, but we like it.'

'Though God knows what the guests must think sometimes,' Nora grinned, heading out of the room. 'We need some clean tablecloths. Back in a sec.'

Maureen stood thinking for a moment, then walked over to Sean. 'I want to speak to you, Sean, about everything you've done — the rooms and everything. I don't know how I can ever repay you.'

Sean looked offended. 'Who said we wanted repaying? You're family, Maureen. You may not want us to be, but we are.' His smile was genuine. 'So stop apologising. Our home is your home. Okay?'

Maureen was deeply touched by the sincerity of his words. 'You know,' she said, 'for a time I was jealous of you and Nora. When I came here last time, I was jealous of your closeness, and your happiness. But now, I'm not jealous. I'm just grateful. I'd forgotten what a nice feeling it is to be included.'

Sean smiled gently. '*Everyone* likes to be included, Maureen. That's what life and living is all about.'

# TWENTY-SIX

Liza slept heavily, but she awoke to find the morning sun streaming into the room.

She opened her eyes with a startled movement. Her bed was in the Prep ward where the light had suddenly changed as a nurse pulled back the drawn drapes on the main ward's windows to let in the light of day.

'Nurse!'

A second nurse walked in carrying a cup of tea. 'Good morning.'

Liza jerked upright, but the nurse smiled at her reassuringly. 'Jamie's fine. He slept like a log.'


Michael Docherty was overseeing a noisy 'playtime' when he received the call from Liza on his mobile.

'You'll have to speak up,' Michael said loudly. 'I'm out in the playground — Donal! You punch him and I'll punch you back!' Then into the phone, 'You what? He's had it?' When?'

Liza knew it was a difficult time to speak to him, but she couldn't contain her excitement.

'Last night. There was nothing to it. It just drips in through the Hickman line ... No, he's as right as

253

rain. He's sitting here next to me sucking an ice lolly.'

'Brilliant!' Relieved and delighted, Michael bent to tie up a kid's shoe lace. 'So how long before he starts to feel any effects?'

'Soon,' Liza replied. 'His counts are dropping and his mouth's getting sore. Listen, Michael, I know about the donor. I know it was Brian Lessing.'

The smile left Michael's face. 'Liza, I'm sorry, I—'

'Don't deny it. I just wanted to thank you, for persuading him.'

'It wasn't me who persuaded him. It was his own decision. His and his mother's — Donal! I warned you, Donal!'

Liza could hear a noisy commotion in the background. Michael's voice came back on the line. 'Listen, Liza, I've got to go. You're doing grand. Hang in there.'

Michael cut the connection and hurried over to the fight that had broken out in the corner of the yard.

Sean Mullen was feeling the effects of a slight hangover. He stood in the back garden muttering his usual complaint. 'If I'm not working at bleedin' work, I'm working at bleedin' home.'

He propped the ladder against the wall and looked at Brian. 'Now if you hold the ladder for me,

Brian, I'll climb up and see if there *is* anything blocking the guttering. Half the time she makes these things up just to keep me busy.'

Bridget appeared carrying a large bouquet of flowers. 'Well, now. You must have a little turtle dove, Brian.'

'For me?' Brian looked disbelieving.

'They must be from that girlfriend of yours in Germany,' Bridget beamed. 'How romantic. Sending you flowers.'

Brian smiled as he reached for the card and opened the envelope … a mixture of surprise and disappointment on his face as he read the words.

'Ah, let's see …' Bridget peered and read, *God bless you. Liza Becker.*

She looked at Brian. 'The boy's mother — that was nice of her.'

'She wasn't supposed to know I was the donor,' Brian said, then shrugged, because her knowing didn't matter anymore. Right now Brian had another woman and child on his mind, and all he really wanted to do was get back to Germany and Eva.


Michael Docherty arrived at the Mullens an hour later.

'Lunch break,' he explained to Maureen. 'I just wanted you to know that Jamie's had the actual transplant. Last night. And everything looks fine. I'm on my way to the hospital now.'

A smile of relief lit up Maureen's blue eyes. 'That's great news. Brian will be pleased. He's upstairs packing at the moment.' Maureen lowered her voice and seemed to speak for his ears only. 'We're not leaving until tomorrow but I think Brian is hoping to persuade us to go back tonight.'

Michael hesitated. 'Are you sure you don't want to meet Liza? I know she'd like to thank you personally.'

'No, no,' Maureen said too quickly for politeness. 'No, there's still a lot of things I need to do before I leave.'

Michael accepted defeat courteously. 'Well, thank you again. And thank Brian and Maeve for me also. Say goodbye to them for me.'

Maureen gazed at him thoughtfully. 'Liza and you … you must be very close.'

'Close?' Michael smiled at the euphemism. 'Not like you think. I had a few problems a way back. She helped. We're friends. Good friends. We sing in the same choir.'

When Maureen just stood there, looking at him shrewdly, Michael felt the need to explain further.

'She used to help out part-time at the school. That's how we met. Then when Jamie came along it seemed only natural for him to go there. He's a great kid.'

'Did you know my husband?'

'No. Only in passing. He was ...' Michael's face reddened with embarrassment, 'always away on business.'

'Do you know how they met? Him and her?'

Michael was beginning to feel uncomfortable. 'I think it was at a business seminar. He was advising small companies about software applications. She was trying to set up her own knitwear design company.'

'Excuse me,' Bridget butted in. 'Maureen. That German. The accountant fella. He's on the phone downstairs. Wants to speak to you urgently, he says.'

Maureen could have screamed blue fury at both Hans and Bridget for interrupting — 'Tell him I'll ring him back, will you, Bridget. Thanks.'

An awkward moment as she waited for Bridget to go. A moment long enough to make her realise that now was not the time, and this doorstep was not the place. And what difference would knowing make now. The dead could not be resurrected and the truth could not be changed.

'I'm sorry,' she said to Michael Docherty. 'I shouldn't have asked you those questions.'

'That's okay. But, Maureen, why don't you ask Liza yourself?'

'No.'

'Liza is desperate for answers too.'

Once again Maureen seemed to be gazing at him in a strange way, as if observing a fool.

257

'Goodbye Michael.'

Michael stood and watched her as she turned and went inside, her manner calm and dignified.

She had unsettled him somehow … Why did he always get the feeling that she knew something about Liza that he did not?

When Maureen returned to the kitchen, Sean, Nora and Maeve were seated at the table having their lunch. A place was set for Maureen, another for Brian.

'More good news,' Maureen said. 'That was Michael Docherty at the door. Came to tell us Jamie had the transplant last night, and all seems to be working well.'

Sean put down his knife and fork. 'Now that's the *best* news of all.'

Maeve was staring at her mother with tears in her eyes. 'Can I go up and tell Brian, Mum? *Please* let me be the one to tell him?'

'Of course you can, love. And tell him Bridget has his lunch waiting.'

Once Maeve had gone, Maureen turned to Bridget, about to apologise for her sharp manner at the front door, but Bridget gave her no chance. She clutched Maureen's arm and looked at her guiltily.

'Tell you what but, Maureen. That German accountant fella. He's rung a few times over the last few days, but with all the goings-on at the hospital and everything, I forgot to tell you.'

Maureen shrugged. 'It doesn't matter. Probably just ringing with some more bad news about the bank.'

'That's not all but,' Bridget went on anxiously. 'I think, because of me forgetting to give you any of his messages, and now you being too busy talking to another man ... I think he's got fed up phoning you.'

'What do you mean?'

'He said to tell you he'll be on the next flight over here. Said he was ringing from the airport in Düsseldorf . Said he had something very important to tell you. Said you'll be very pleased.'

'Coming here?' Maureen was astounded. 'Didn't you tell him I was going back tomorrow?'

'I didn't get a chance! As soon as I told him you couldn't come to the phone he said he was in the airport and from then on he did all the talking. I couldn't get a word in edgeways. Not a word!'

'My God,' Sean exclaimed, almost with reverence. 'This German must be a rare genius if he managed to keep you quiet, Mother. What did you say his name was, Maureen — Einstein?'

'Hans Reiner.'

Bridget grunted, determined to re-establish her authority and have the last word as always. 'Hans Reiner? Not a very German name, is it? Sounds more like a fancy French name to me.'

'French?'

'Aye, French. Like that husband of our own dear

and departed Grace Kelly. Prince Reiner of Monaco.'

Maureen smiled faintly, sitting down at the table and removing the layer of cling-film from her plate of chicken salad. 'Will you pass the salt please, Nora?'

'Sure that's *Rainier*,' Sean said suddenly, looking up from his plate. 'Prince Rainier of Monaco. A different name entirely to Reiner.'

But Bridget's eradicable belief in her own authority and having the last word remained intact, because she had already left the room.


Hans arrived later that evening.

Bridget led him directly into the conservatory where Maureen was sitting alone. 'Maureen,' she said with a lively tone in her voice. 'You have a visitor.'

Hans followed, smiling rather stiffly. 'Maureen, please forgive me for just arriving like this.'

Maureen rose and took his outstretched hand in hers. 'Hans, what on earth made you come here?'

'Right,' said Bridget, 'I'll check if we've got any rooms vacant, but I don't think we have, so God knows where we're going to put you. Probably the Town House again.'

Hans and Maureen sat down together. Hans was very excited at seeing her again but tried to hide it, endeavouring with great effort to compose his features.

'The old lady,' he said, 'she told me on the phone all about your troubles here. About the sick boy and how Maeve ... and then Brian ... Well, that's when I knew I had to ask you ...' He considered her with a look of pure indulgence. 'Maureen, you know how much I care for you?'

Maureen struggled with the tumult in her breast. 'Is that why you came here, Hans? To tell me that you care for me?'

'No, not only that. I wanted also to reassure you. About everything at home. Nothing for you to worry about. It was just a legal technicality. A summons for a court hearing about repossessing the house. But there's nothing to worry —'

'A summons?' she said, shocked. 'I didn't know anything about a summons for a court hearing.'

'Don't worry. Everything's fine.'

'Fine? I'm about to go to court to have my house repossessed and I didn't know a thing about it.'

'Maureen, there's no question of you going to court. Or of you losing the house. I've managed to work something out with the Bank.'

'What?'

'I have personally guaranteed the debt.'

Hans laughed, very pleased with himself. 'Now don't go all independent on me. It will be just like a loan. Between you and I.'

'No!'

'No?' Confounded, Hans stared at her. 'Maureen! What's the matter?'

'Hans, let's get this straight. I'm a grown-up woman with two grown-up children. I can make my own decisions.'

'Of course, but you have had a very tough time —'

'Hans, please, don't patronise me. I'm not a fool, and I'm not incapable. And I don't want your money.'

'What?'

'I'm sorry, Hans, but I don't want to be in hock to anyone — not for anything — never again.'

Cold, rigid, Hans stared at her, aware of her emphasis on the word 'anything'.

'I'm not trying to buy you, Maureen.'

Maureen looked him directly in the eyes and decided to be brutally honest.

'Yes, you are, Hans. Buy my house, and you will own me. That's what you think, and that's what you have decided. And now you come here expecting me to be grateful. Expecting me to lay my head on your manly shoulder in blessed relief. But you thought wrong, Hans, because I have nothing you can buy.'

Hans was astounded. 'So you don't care if you lose your home?'

'Yes, I do care if I lose it. But I'm not ready to exchange it.'

Hans could see she was determined. He gave her a look of bitter resentment. 'Very well.'

He stood up to leave. 'The bank will be closed now. So, you have until tomorrow to change your mind. If you do, you only have to say. I will ask the old lady to find me somewhere else to stay tonight.'

When he had gone, Maureen sat for a long time in deep thought, remembering back through all those long and faithful wifely years when she would have bitten off her own tongue rather than hurt or give offence to anyone.

# TWENTY-SEVEN

Liza sat by Jamie's bed watching the television suspended outside his room. She had waited until he had fallen asleep before gently removing the remote control from his hands and switching over from the cartoon channel to a movie on Sky.

After so much agonising and worry and tension, it was nice now to be able to relax and be entertained by Meg Ryan and Tom Hanks in *Sleepless in Seattle*.

She adjusted her position on the chair and snuggled down with her head on the pillow beside Jamie's; lying cheek-to-cheek in close comfort with her sleeping darling, while smiling at the frustrated antics of Tom Hanks who was trying to cope with a small son who desperately wanted his lonely dad to find a new partner.

Her hands limp upon the bed, her eyes drowsy with tiredness, she dozed into a dreamy sleep that lasted until after the end of the movie.

Every so often the nurse had glanced in through the window at her, wondering if she should disturb her, coax her to go to her own bed. But she was used to Mrs Becker now, popping in to see Jamie at all hours of the night, moving about his room in her sterile suit and overslippers, bending to feel his temperature, swab his face, wipe Dettol over every surface. No wonder she was exhausted.

From a switch outside the room, the nurse turned off the television. The isolation room was now in semi-darkness. Only the small angled lamp illuminated Liza dozing cheek-to-cheek beside her sleeping son.

Liza awoke with the feeling of hot tears rolling down her face. She opened her eyes slowly. Why was she crying? And why was it so hot?

Still only half-awake, she lifted her head and saw Jamie's face drenched in sweat ... Her hand touched his face, arms, chest — he was burning as hot as an oven. She checked his pulse ...

She was already screaming when her hand hit the emergency button. '*Nurse! Nurse!*'

Everything that followed she perceived through a red haze, as if in some kind of delirium, watching the panic of the nurses and the rushed arrival of a doctor wearing a white coat and a stethoscope who strapped a blood pressure cuff on Jamie's left arm, followed by Dr Brady who glanced at the wall monitors and immediately started snapping out orders ...

The rest was a nightmare that she watched and listened to behind a veil of horror. Time was suspended. All the voices were distorted. Being ushered into another room. A nurse, speaking to her, handing her a cup of tea that she sipped once and then dropped from her shaking hands onto the floor. Looking down at the smashed pieces. Hearing the silence. Looking up at the pale face of Dr Brady in the doorway ... seeing the sorrow and defeat in his eyes.

She walked back into the isolation room and stood looking down at Jamie, still fast asleep, his mind far away in a childish dream from which he would never awaken.

Dr Brady was gently speaking to her.

She gave no answer.

Dr Brady, Brendan the haemotologist, and many of the other hospital and nursing staff stood behind her in the pews of the church.

Liza stood passive, listening to the choir of St Mary's School in Bray singing in beautiful harmony, replacing a new name in an old song.

> *Now he lives far away o'er the mountains*
> *Where the little birds sing in the trees*
> *In a cottage all covered with ivy*
> *My Jamie is waiting for me ...*

After the church service, out in the green graveyard, she remained composed and dignified, as if nothing could hurt her now. Nurses and neighbours may cry, but she did not. The priest and congregation may pray, but she would not. All hope was gone now. She didn't need God anymore.

Michael Docherty touched her arm in silent signal. Everyone was waiting for her.

She stepped forward and placed a spray of flowers onto the small coffin, stepping back to feel Michael's comforting arm around her as she stood watching the coffin being lowered from view.

It was over.

She turned to leave, and only then did she notice the three people standing slightly apart from the other mourners. She stood to stare at them, a faint smile on her pale face.

Maeve hesitated only for a second, then ran over and gave Liza a tight hug of comfort, tears spilling down her face.

Liza ended up comforting the girl. And then, more hesitantly, her brother came over — the two of them — joining her in her sorrow. Two young people who had tried so hard to help Jamie. All in vain.

Liza's look of gratitude encompassed them both. 'You will come back to the house now, won't you?' she said. 'With the others?' Her eyes moved up to Brian, so like his father. 'I would like to get to know you better.'

Maeve and Brian glanced at each other. How could they say no?

'We'd love to,' Maeve said.

'And your mother? Will she come?'

Only then did Brian and Maeve look back to where they had left their mother standing apart and alone. But now there was no sign of her.

Maureen had gone.

Maureen wandered alone for hours along the seafront in Bray, staring at the rocks pushing out to the sea, and then further beyond to the distant horizon.

She walked in staring remoteness, her hands in her pockets, wondering why life was such a confusing business, and why so many hopes for the boy had fallen into the void.

She watched the gushing white foam of the rushing sea and felt a final, devastating wave of anger and anguish, and regret for her own hardness. A blade of shame, as sharp as a surgeon's scalpel cutting through her. How hard to remember now all those telephone calls from Michael Docherty begging her to help the boy. How could she have been so cruelly foolish to allow her rage against James and Liza Becker prevent her from doing the right thing straight away. And if she had — would it have changed things? Or would Jamie still have died?

That was something she would never know. Something she would always have to wonder about.

Home. She turned away from the sea. Home was the only place she wanted to be now, not the one in

Germany, but the nearer home of the Mullens'
kitchen.

Inside Liza's house, as is usual at funerals, the
mourners were all trying to cheer each other up.

Michael Docherty was the host, pacing the
rooms making sure everyone had all the refreshment
they needed. He overheard Dr Brady giving an
explanation to the priest.

'Gram Negative Septicaemia. It was always a
risk …'

Passing by the French windows, he saw Liza and
Brian Lessing sitting together at a little wrought iron
table in the corner of the garden. Liza looked calm,
and very much in control of her emotions. Michael
decided it might be wise at this moment to leave
them alone.

'Oh, Michael didn't tell me you were the donor,'
Liza was saying to Brian. 'I saw you through the
window.'

Brian was confused. 'Where? At the hospital?'

'Yes. It was just luck.' She smiled. 'You were
hobbling a bit.'

'Yeah. Like an old man. I think the painkillers
were beginning to wear off.'

'Was it painful? I'm sorry, I hadn't even thought —'

'No. It was nothing. Honestly. A slight
discomfort. Nothing more than that.'

269

Liza suddenly smirked. 'It's funny how polite we all are to each other, isn't it?'

Brian looked at her directly, his voice very low. 'All I can say is I'm sorry … I don't know what else to say.'

Liza leaned towards him, a strange compassion in her eyes. 'It wasn't your fault,' she said strongly. 'I want you to understand that. Without you, we wouldn't have had any chance at all.'

'But I could have come forward sooner.'

'It would have made no difference if you had,' Liza replied honestly. 'That's the sad truth of it.'

That evening, once all the mourners had gone, the house seemed very quiet; deathly so.

Michael Docherty stood over a pile of dishes in the sink, diligently washing up. Liza had gone upstairs to rest, something he had urged her to do.

But now, alone with his grief and his anger, Michael suddenly paused, listening to the echoing silence of the house, feeling no longer able to resist it.

Ignoring his wet hands, he turned to the assembly of bottles on the table and lifted the whiskey. Very deliberately he poured a large shot into a glass, and downed it in one.

'Michael — what are you *doing*?'

He turned round to be confronted by Liza, white-faced with anger.

Michael shrugged. 'It's just one drink, okay? Days like this call for something a bit stronger than orange juice.'

'Don't you dare blame this on Jamie!'

He was astonished. 'I'm not.'

Liza grabbed up the whiskey bottle and emptied it down the sink.

'Liza, I'm sorry,' Michael said repentantly. 'I don't suppose if I said that I would never touch another drop you'd believe me.'

'Yes, if you swore it. Swear it, Michael. If not for yourself, for Jamie.'

'I swear it, Liza. For Jamie.'

Liza turned back to the table, sitting down suddenly, very tired.

'No one failed Jamie, Michael. Not you. Not Brian Lessing … Not even Maureen Lessing. She did what she could in the end. If anyone failed Jamie, it was me.'

'You! No mother could have done more for her son.'

'You don't understand. I lied, Michael. I lied to you. And I lied to myself.'

She stared blankly in front of her, speaking in the flat voice which heralds something bad or sad that must sooner or later be told.

'I always knew about James's wife and family. His *real* family. I knew from the beginning. I wasn't stupid.'

'You knew he was married?' Michael was stunned by her admission. 'So why didn't you stop it. Why didn't you at least *do something* about it?'

'I did do something,' Liza replied flatly. 'I deliberately got pregnant.'

'What?'

'I can still remember the panic in James's eyes when I told him I was pregnant. He couldn't speak. It must have been his worst nightmare. There were many times afterwards when I hated him for that. He was happy to sleep with me, but not to have a child with me.'

Michael did not speak, yet a faint tinge of disillusionment shadowed his eyes.

'I wanted to force James to choose me instead of her, you see. His wife. She meant nothing to me. I wanted to force him to choose Jamie instead of his other two children. I never cared about them. But I knew he did. So I tried every way I could to force him to leave them. None of it worked ... But then, when Jamie got ill ... I suppose I knew he only stayed because of Jamie's illness.'

There was a pitiful silence.

'I used my sick son for my own selfish greed. I sacrificed my son, for my own greed. And that's why God took him from me. He took my little boy to punish me.'

Michael couldn't withhold a groan of anger. 'No, Liza! If you're going to face up to the truth now — then face *all* of it. Jamie had an illness. A blood condition that is sadly common in a lot of children. His leukaemia was not your fault — no more than it's the fault of any parent with a child suffering from the disease. Christ, how can you say that!'

'But many of those children are saved, aren't they, Michael? Yet Jamie wasn't saved. No matter how hard we all tried. No, in the end God turned his back on me. And now I'm turning my back on him.'

She stood up to leave — Michael caught her arm. 'You don't mean that, Liza. Don't throw away your faith now. Not when you need it most.'

'*What* faith? Any faith I had was for my little boy! What use have I for it now?'

She turned and walked out of the room. He heard her footsteps on the stairs, her bedroom door closing.

Michael turned and lifted his coat to leave, feeling in his heart a searing pity for her. Whatever else she had done, she had just lost her son. And that was pain enough for any woman.

Outside on the road, Michael paused to look up at Liza's bedroom window. The light had not been switched on. She had lain down in the darkness, probably without getting undressed.

Yet, despite all the things he had heard this night, much of which still confused him, Michael was certain of only one thing — Liza needed his friendship now more than ever. His friendship and his love.

# TWENTY-EIGHT

A last visit before leaving, a final journey out to Bray.

Maureen walked slowly along the meandering grey paths of the cemetery. A distant view of the mountains provided a serene backdrop to this place, but she did not find it peaceful, rather shadeless and sad. For the old the final rest was probably welcome, but not for a child who loved trikes and football and television shows.

At Jamie's grave she stood staring down, struggling with her own sorrow, and then remembering something Father Cornelius had said gently to her on the telephone the night before; a quote probably from the Bible, or maybe even Shakespeare.

*'Our bones may moulder and become the earth of the fields but our spirit flies forth and lives on high in a condition of glorious brightness.'*

She hoped so. She really hoped young Jamie was flying high somewhere with his guardian angel, happily free of platelet-pumps and chemotherapy and all the other things that had blighted his young life.

Some of the flowers on the grave were already

wilting in the heat. Such a pity, they had looked so beautiful yesterday. She wondered if she could delay their doom by supplying them with water.

She looked around her; there was a tap at the end of the path and beside it an old rusting watering can.

She made her way over to the watering can and filled it from the tap, listening to the water clanging inside the old metal. She turned back to the grave.

A woman stood in her way. Maureen had not heard her approaching footsteps, and now both women stood looking at each other, not knowing how to breach the chasm between them.

'I just wanted to pay my respects,' Maureen said, an embarrassed flush on her face. Then nodding at the can in her hand. 'The flowers, they're wilting.'

'It's hot,' Liza said. 'But I wanted fresh flowers only, I didn't want wreaths.'

Maureen stood looking at her, feeling desperately sorry for her, yet knowing she could never like this woman.

'I'm sorry,' she said quickly, putting down the watering can. 'I shouldn't have come.'

'No.' Liza said. 'No, it was good of you … You are very kind.' She took the watering can from Maureen's hand and tried to smile. 'Will you help me with the flowers?'

Maureen slowly followed her to the grave.

'I want you to know,' Maureen said, her voice trembling with emotion, 'About Jamie. I never — I didn't want this to happen. If I could change things, believe me, I would.'

'You weren't to blame.'

Liza knelt and began carefully tending the flowers. 'It's strange now to have so much time on my hands. I was always so busy before. What with the tablets and hospital visits and everything. It gives you something to do. It's a long wait, you see. When they're ill. A long time to be frightened. Now I'm not frightened any more.'

'Have you thought about what you'll do now?'

'I don't know. Sell the house? Move?' Liza shrugged. 'Michael reckons you can't run away from it. I told him, why would I want to do that? Grief's the only thing I've got left now. There's a sort of comfort in it.'

Maureen had an inexplicable impulse to retreat. But first, she knew she needed to apologise for the first time they had met. 'It was wrong of me,' she said, 'telling you like that, about James being dead. I thought ... but Michael insists that James lied to you too.'

'We all lie,' Liza replied.

'I know now that I lied to myself,' Maureen confessed. 'I thought I loved James. Now I know that I didn't love him, not really. Not like you did. No, these past years James and I had slowly grown apart, you see. People do if they're not careful.'

Liza's strange pale smile deepened. 'At least you

didn't know the truth. I did ... but I still went on with it.'

'You knew?'

'No more lies.' Liza said. 'I think we've both had enough lies to last a lifetime.' She looked at Maureen. 'I'm sorry for what I did to you and your family. Believe me, I'm sorry.'

Maureen couldn't answer her.

Liza stared down at the flowers. 'They'll be fine now,' she said softly. 'I've always loved flowers. It comes from being brought up in the Tyrol. All those meadows of wild flowers. My mother, she had a beautiful garden. She always said it was hard work but worth it. As if God was making us tend them with our tears. A bit like children.'

'I have to go,' Maureen said apologetically. 'I'm flying back to Germany this afternoon.'

Liza stood up, her hands clasping the watering can. 'Our two families, we have shared so much these past few weeks ... but you and I, we could never be friends, could we?'

Maureen shook her head silently; some things were just not realistic or possible.

For a moment Liza looked vaguely disconcerted. 'Will you say goodbye to Brian and Maeve for me?'

'Yes,' Maureen agreed. 'I'll tell them.'

'Jamie would have been proud of them, ' Liza said softly. 'If he had known who they were, and what they tried to do for him.' She reached out and touched Maureen's arm. 'Thank you.'

Maureen could only nod, tears in her eyes as she turned and walked away.

When she reached the end of the path she glanced back and saw Liza Becker, motionless, standing where she had left her, her body fixed in that same stance, straight and unbending, the same tense look on her white face.

Maureen continued walking down the pathway without looking back. A new wave of confusion swept over her. All this, and what had any of them gained? All of it had resulted in devastating loss, and what was the point of it?

'Oh, Lord,' she whispered with simple pleading. 'If nothing else, let me learn something from this.'

Yet, even now, she knew that Liza Becker would be all right and come through this. You didn't have to be a psychic or an astrologer to see the future already paved for her. She would be comforted in her grief by Michael Docherty. The loss of Jamie a sorrow they would both share intimately, finally leading to marriage and more children, a new family. Jamie's photograph always on display, never to be forgotten.

Maureen could see it all, so clearly. Yet what of her own future? What there?

Her eyes wandered over the cemetery and its acres of headstones and suddenly she realised it didn't matter. Whatever the future held she would make the best of it and enjoy it.

Brian must have seen her from the window, heard the taxi. She was paying off the driver when he rushed out of the Mullens front door to greet her, a smile of pure joy on his face.

'Mum, I want you to be the first to know — Eva and I — we've sorted everything out. And she's decided to keep the baby.'

'Oh, Brian, that's wonderful!' Maureen reached up and hugged him tightly. Some good news at last!

'That's great, Brian, really great ... Sure Eva's almost one of the family already,' she said, laughing. All the time she has spent in our house.'

Brian's joy faded slightly. 'About the house —'

'Ah, feck the house!' Maureen said brightly, in a fair imitation of Bridget. 'As soon as we get back I'm going to sell it and clear off all our debts. It's not a home anymore. It's just bricks and mortar, a huge mass of stone around our necks. *We're* the family, Brian, not the bloody house.'

She squeezed his arm and grinned as they walked indoors. 'I'll rent a nice flat maybe, for me and Maeve. Start again.'

Nora said to her later. 'And you could maybe even move back to Ireland again. Renting a place here is as easy as renting a place there.'

Maureen laughed. 'Oh, I don't know. As much as I love dear old Dublin, I'm still very fond of dear old Düsseldorf.'

The Aer Lingus jet roared its way up into the brilliant cloudless sky, arcing out across the Irish Sea ... leaving behind the coastline and the town of Bray, and the distant figure of a woman in a little churchyard on the hill, still carefully tending the swathe of flowers blanketing a small grave.